1

1 Thessalonians 4:11-12
Make it your ambition to lead a quiet life, to mind your own
business and to work with your hands, just as we told you, so
that your daily life may win the respect of outsiders and so
that you will not be dependent on anybody.

Cover photo – Rosalyn Stowell.   Thanks to Kara Stowell for proof reading, any remaining mistakes are my own.

Other books by Rosalyn Stowell
Don't Use A Chainsaw In The Kitchen – How-to and Cookbook
PAW (Post Apocalyptic World) Trilogy
The Beginning – Book 1
The Dark of Night – Book 2
The Dawn – Book 3
Alaskan Gold – novel, romance
Alaskan Alibi – novel, suspense
Stikine – novel, suspense
Cold Gold – novel, suspense
Klondike – novel, historical
A Head Of The Game – novel, serial killer
A Rat by Any Other Name….SHTF novel
Trouble In Paradise…..A Paradise, Alaska novel

Trouble in Paradise

A Paradise, Alaska novel
By
Rosalyn Stowell

Chapter 1

Paradise, Alaska came by its name in the usual way. Someone, sick and tired of the greed, hustle and bustle of life in a city somewhere took off into the Wilderness with a pack on his back and a vow to never return to his former life. He wandered around a lot, finally stumbled and almost fell, picked up a gold nugget, greed jumped right back into his hip pocket and stayed firmly glued.

Gold! He could be rich. Whatever girl that threw him over for a richer/handsomer/older man would sit up and take notice now and wish she was with him instead of with her not quite so rich/no longer handsome/old man. He could afford to flaunt his wealth and pick one of the new crop of debutantes to grace his life and hang on his arm when they walked out in public.

Then he could build a town the way he wanted it to be and have all the things he left behind.

As so many things do, the dream turned out to be so much better than the reality. Reality hit when someone took a shot at him as he stepped out into the street from his hotel a few days after arriving. The fact that they missed was the good news but he was so scared he messed himself and fell into the horse trough near the hitching post in front of the fancy hotel he was staying at, in Seattle.

As bystanders assisted him out of the murky water, someone caught a whiff of him and dropped his arm, stepping back and fanning the air in front of his face.

The newspaper reporter that he was supposed to meet showed up about then and trailed along downwind of him back into the hotel as he trailed water and unmentionable crud in his wake through the posh lobby. The bell captain was ringing for cleanup before he even reached his room. Oh, someone was going to pay and they were going to pay big time for this humiliation. The reporter made the mistake of snickering as they reached his door and he slammed it in his face. Big mistake.

Even though there was never an interview, there was still an article in the next day's paper about the incident, using all the humor and innuendo possible, the reporter had filled out his column and made his point. Don't mess with the media.

The story reached San Francisco on the same boat he did and might never have seen the light of day, except he was checking in the fanciest hotel when someone in the lobby read the article out loud and everyone laughed. The counter clerk was just reading his filled out form and read his name aloud at the same time the room stilled and laughter erupted again. The gentleman starring in our story punched the closest laughing mouth which belonged to one of the pillars of local society. His stay went downhill from there.

By the next morning, the big shot in his own mind was traveling on down to Los Angeles and hoped they had some kind of society that he could pick out a fancy young wife from.

Los Angeles was still little more than a wide spot in the trail to Mexico City but they did have some wealthy Spanish ranchers and what passed as society and no one had a copy of the newspaper, yet, so he set out to pick the cream of the crop for his future wife as fast as possible.

He was about to enter the best hotel in town when a carriage pulled up in the street, not even attempting to pull over and allow traffic through. He stopped to see who had that kind of arrogance. The most beautiful girl he had ever seen stepped out of the carriage onto the arm of a stern looking old man. She was elegant and lovely, a lady to the tips of her toes, he thought.

He doffed his hat and bowed to her as she swept through the doors into the hotel and on to the dining room. She ignored him as was only fitting. No lady would acknowledge a stranger. He immediately decided he was in love and she would be the perfect wife.

In English, her name was Temperance. Her brothers said it should have stopped at Temper. This is what they called her when their Grandfather was not around to hear. He did not see the humor in it and if they were honest about it, he did not see the humor in anything. His only child and heir had recklessly gotten himself killed and left his father to raise 4 orphaned children, a chore the old man would gladly have done without. The only one of them with any backbone was the girl. The three boys were exactly like their father. He wished it were the other way around as the girl was going to be the death of him.

She could outride most of his stockmen and all of her brothers. She could also out cuss them in three languages as he learned while overhearing them practicing behind the barn one day when they were younger and he doubted if she had forgotten any of it in the years since. She had mastered the long stock whip years ago.

He needed to find a husband for her and he wanted it done yesterday. So when the well-dressed audacious Gringo stepped up to him later in the day and asked to speak to him, he granted him a short interview. When he heard the subject matter, he mentally rubbed his hands in glee. Outwardly, he remained stern and unyielding, giving the young man no reason to think he was even willing to think about the subject. After all, this certainly was not the method approved by his generation. Someone lower in each family would approach the other and subtly hint that it was time to form an alliance between the families. Sometimes the two getting married never even met until the day they were wed.

If Temperance had not been on her Grandfather's list of impossible problems needing solved, the young man would have been brushed off without a thought. But just the day before, he caught her wearing men's pants, riding astride across the fields. One of their neighbors also had seen her and she was now being gossiped about in the very best homes. Her chances for a well-connected marriage contract had just gone down the drain. The best he could hope for was a contract with someone outside the area.

But now! Now he had been handed an opportunity on a silver platter. He did not stop to question his own motives too thoroughly, he only knew this was the answer to many fervent prayers on his part. Now to haggle the marriage contract to his advantage. Like most of the big land owners, he never had money, he had land and cattle. What would this affluent looking Gringo have in mind?

When the Gringo offered him a share in his gold mine in Alaska and a sum of money that boggled his mind, he almost broke into a smile. The fool didn't realize he was supposed to pay the bride price as her dowry. This was getting better and better. Not only would he get rid of his biggest headache, he would actually be as wealthy as everyone thought he was.

Visions of shipping his grandsons far off, maybe to Spain, to be educated and get them out of his hair settled in his mind and stayed firmly lodged. Yes, this was his lucky day. The Gringo sat fairly patiently waiting for some sign that he might eventually be successful in his bid for the lovely vision waiting in the other room. He caught a glimpse of her gliding through the room beyond the one they were sitting in and upped his cash offer. The old man didn't even blink.

Just how wealthy was this young fool? Did he really have enough money to keep throwing it away? The old man signaled to his majordomo to bring writing materials and settled in to write out the contract. He didn't want anything to change this man's mind about his granddaughter and he knew it would only be a matter of hours before she did something.

Temperance was fuming beneath her calm exterior. She well knew how to mask her true feelings. That was one of the first lessons any young lady learned. She hated the confinements of being a Lady. Her Father Confessor despaired of her ever marrying and having a family as all young wealthy women were destined to do unless they entered the Church and this one would never be suitable for Church life. He often chided her for her behavior but she just couldn't fit into the mold they all tried shoving her into.

As she slowly walked across the room just beyond the room her Grandfather was entertaining the young man in, she glanced at him and gave him a good looking over under her lowered lashes. It would definitely be unseemly to openly look at the man. It might even earn her another whipping.

He wasn't all that bad to look at, at least he was young. If he would get rid of those silly mutton chop whiskers and allow his hair to lay naturally on his head instead of slicked down and parted ruthlessly in the middle it might be attractive. She had few illusions about why he was here. Her Grandfather couldn't wait to get rid of her. She was just lucky he had enough pride in his family name that he didn't just sell her off to the slave trade.

Once the papers were signed, everything moved at top speed. The groom was impatient to return to his fledgling town and gold mine up in Alaska and her Grandfather was afraid she would allow her prospective husband to see just what kind of woman he was tying himself to for life.

The bans were read in church that Sunday and a special dispensation was given for a speedy marriage. She was sure that cost her Grandfather a healthy amount and expected construction to begin immediately on some new building for the church.

The wedding itself was hastily put together and as soon as the ceremony was over, they were on their way north to catch the ship they were booked on, heading to Alaska.

Their wedding night was postponed until later as they were traveling by carriage over terrible roads, changing horses as they went, never stopping for longer than it took to change out the team and she better have relieved herself while she had the chance or she could suffer to the next stop.

She knew she looked a mess when they boarded the ship but there was no help for it. Trying to look like she had not just spent the last week in a carriage was impossible and they didn't even have time to clean up in a hotel before boarding. Her new husband handed her down from the carriage right on the dock they were leaving from and hurried her along to the ship. The escort her Grandfather had provided unpacked all the trunks and boxes holding her possessions and whatever the old man thought they would need for the trip north and loaded them onto the ship.

As they entered their stateroom, she didn't know what to expect and dread filled her. She would never allow this man she was now tied to for life know just how much she feared him. She held her head high and inspected the room as slowly as she could.

A tap at the door interrupted her slow walk and he opened the door to let a couple of the crew in, carrying more of her trunks and boxes. By the time they finished, the room was filled with only narrow paths between the door and the bed and bathroom. She would have to go through every one of them to make sure nothing perishable was sent down to store in the hold. She didn't even know where a clean dress could be found in this hodge podge.

"Well, Husband, what are we supposed to do with this mess?"

"My guess would be, pick one and send the rest down to storage unless you like living in a cave and you can call me Luke. I'm not sure if I would remember and answer to Husband."

So, maybe he did have some humor in him, she thought, maybe we can make this work. Not like there was a lot of choice, since she was now his legal possession just as surely as if he had bid on her on the block.

Luke left the stateroom shortly after that and Temperance was alone with her pile of trunks. She started opening them and finally found one that contained day dresses then picked one of the dressier ones from another trunk to keep out for evening wear at dinner. Each trunk had the appropriate underclothes for the outfits, so she rang for someone to remove the rest of the luggage to storage. Then she rang again for a bath.

She was truly going to miss her maid. She didn't know how she was going to button or unbutton any of these dresses as they all buttoned or hooked up the back.

She was gratified to see a woman in the hallway and didn't hesitate to ask for help. The woman looked at her oddly but agreed to help her.

"I'm sorry to ask you for assistance, but I had to leave my maid at home and I just can't reach any of the fasteners on my dresses. Whoever designed women's clothes should be drawn and quartered." Temperance muttered.

The woman laughed. "I don't mind helping, but I really am not suitable to be helping you, I work in the entertainment field."

"Oh, that must be interesting. Do you sing?"

"Um, no. I really am not suitable to be even speaking to you. Anyone seeing me here would probably just throw me overboard. Really, I better be going and I will see if I can find your husband to come help fasten you back up after your bath," the woman looked down and edged toward the door.

"Don't go. I have no one to talk to and I don't see why we can't be friends. I won't know anyone in Alaska and I don't even know my husband. We just got married and tonight will probably be my actual wedding night and I have no idea what to expect."

"Oh damn. Why do people think it is right to marry off girls without a clue? Look, Honey, I'm going to tell you what to expect and how to take care of yourself. Don't ever tell anyone I did this as I would probably be tarred and feathered, but you should know a few things."

Temperance listened wide eyed and blushed often, but was grateful someone was taking the time to explain a good many things to her. No matter what this woman said, Temperance considered her a friend and hoped they could continue being friends in Alaska.

Chapter 2

Once Temperance was dressed again, her new friend eased out the door. On impulse, Temperance hugged her and asked if she could come talk to her again.

The woman again told her she was unsuitable company for decent women and Temperance stamped her foot, saying she was so tired of everyone telling her what and who she could associate with. The woman smiled at her and told her that her name was Charity.

Temperance was feeling a little odd by dinner time but dressed for dinner in her lovely evening dress. Charity stopped by to fasten the back of the gown for her, then hurried on her way, saying she had an appointment.

Luke met her in the hall and complimented her on how nice she looked, then gave her his arm and escorted her into the dining room. They were seated at the Captains table and the service was lovely. Temperance wasn't very hungry and only nibbled at her dinner. Luke appeared to not have much appetite either. As they excused themselves to return to their room, the ship swayed more than it had earlier in the day.

As she readied herself for bed, after Luke gallantly unbuttoned the back of her gown, then left the room, she told herself she could do this. She didn't fully believe everything Charity had told her, but why take chances? She wouldn't panic. After all, people had been doing this forever and no one had died of shock, as far as she knew. She felt slightly ill as she reached the bed, but thought it was just nerves. When she stretched out on the bed, the room seemed to whirl slowly around her. She raced for the bathroom and barely made the commode.

When Luke returned, expecting to find his wife waiting for him, she was still hunched over the commode, retching her last several meals up. He wasn't feeling too great himself and in short order, they were taking turns using the commode. Finally, neither had anything left to heave up and they helped each other to the bed. They were both too ill to consider any of the incredible things Charity had told her about and alternated dozing and running to the commode again, most of the night. She was sure they were both going to die, right there, on that ship.

When there was a light tapping on their door the following morning, they both moaned and he was still gentleman enough to answer the door. A man holding a tray of delicious smelling breakfast stood there, smiling and asking if they would care for breakfast. Luke rushed to the bathroom and was just about through heaving when the odor of the food reached Temperance. She made a mad dash for the commode and almost fell over Luke, trying not to throw up on the floor or him.

The man at the door laughed and said something about sea legs and closed their door. No one in there would be wanting this very nice breakfast sent down for the newlyweds.

Luke and Temperance were both wishing they could manage to get up, get dressed and get out of this smelly room for a while. Fresh air on deck sounded wonderful, but neither one could manage to dress themselves.

Charity stopped by a couple of hours later and found them both still miserable, still cocooned in their dark smelly room. She brought a basin of water to the bed and washed Temperance's hands and face, then helped her dress in a nice day dress and helped her leave the room. She stuck her head back in the door and told Luke she would send one of the crew back to assist him. Then she would have the room cleaned and aired out.

Luke didn't have a clue who the pretty, bossy woman was, but he was grateful to her for helping them out and taking Temperance up on deck. The tap on the door announced the arrival of some help for him. The man was helpful and efficient and soon had Luke cleaned up and on his way on deck. His legs felt wobbly and he certainly hoped they both felt better soon.

One of the crew pointed out his wife, seated by herself in a deck chair with a robe over her to ward off any chill from the sea air.

"Where did the lady go that was helping you? That was certainly nice of her to come in and help out." Luke asked.

"She wouldn't come on out with me, she said people would get the wrong idea and I needed to not be seen with her. But I like her. Maybe we can do something to help her out. She has been helping me dress and undress as I don't have my maid with me anymore."

Luke plopped down in a chair beside her. A maid, she needed a maid to help her dress. He never gave a thought to all those rows of tiny buttons or hooks up the back of her dresses. Where in the word would he find a woman in Alaska that would be willing to move in and be a maid for his new wife? Maids were in short supply in Alaska, to put it mildly. He would ask the woman, Charity.

When he asked one of the crew men about a passenger named Charity, the man gave him a funny look and mumbled something about a newly married man shouldn't already be looking for that sort and walked off, leaving Luke with a bemused expression on his face.

He finally found Charity sitting at a table in the dining room playing a hand of solitaire. He asked if he could join her and she asked if he was sure. Then nodded yes.

"You should know before you are seen with me that I usually work in saloons. I felt sorry for your wife and gave her a hand, but neither of you should be seen with me. It will not help your reputations any," she told him.

"I'm not worried about my reputation and I am sure nothing my wife could do would tarnish hers. I am thankful you had sense enough to give her a hand. I didn't even think that she would need a maid for all those fancy clothes her family sent her up here with. I'm afraid she is going to freeze to death this winter unless I manage to get my home finished before then. I wanted my wife to be here to oversee exactly what she would want in her home. I see now that I really didn't know what I would be asking of a delicately raised young woman."

Charity wondered just how well he knew his new wife, as while they were talking, the woman she had met didn't seem exactly like the delicate gentle woman this young man was describing. Yes, she was innocent in the ways of the world, but she was ranch raised and not a shrinking violet.

Luke asked Charity if she would assist his wife in dressing and undressing for the rest of the trip, as she knew a lot more about that stuff than he did and he wasn't sure whether or not Temperance would appreciate his trying to help.

Charity again tried to dissuade him from having her associate with them but he was adamant. She was the only other woman on board that he knew of and it would be a help to his wife. What anyone else thought was unimportant.

The fresh air did wonders for Temperance and Luke and by evening, they were ready to try dining in the dining room yet again. Luke shrugged into his evening jacket and tie and left as Charity showed up to help Temperance dress for dinner. The room was close and Charity hurried over to open an outside porthole to let in some fresh air. Temperance started looking better almost immediately.

"How about we just leave that open? I know they tell us to keep them closed, but it is so much nicer in here when the air is fresh and I can see you turning green again when it is closed. So unless you plan on sleeping on deck, I would suggest leaving it open."

Temperance agreed and they finished up her hair.
Charity was very good at arranging it so it looked better
than she could remember ever looking. She again
renewed her invitation to dine with them this evening and
Charity again refused. She told her that she had finally
agreed with Luke to assist her in dressing but it really
would not be good for them to be seen together.

Temperance was in a mood by the time she reached the
dining room and found Luke already inside, talking to a
group of men. She stood in the doorway until one of the
men pointed her out to Luke, then he walked over to
escort her to their table. She wasn't happy that her new
friend couldn't join them for dinner and evidently Luke
found the company of the other men more comfortable
than being her escort. She knew how to act the regal
haughty lady and did an admirable job of it all evening.

When she overheard someone talking about the soiled
dove traveling with them, she saw red. She had a fan and
she knew how to use it. She flicked the man standing
behind her on the edge of his ear, almost drawing blood
with the sharp edge of her fan and informed him he was a
boor for even mentioning such a thing and in the hearing
of a lady.

She asked the Captain to excuse her, she flicked Luke
on the arm with her fan, not quite as hard as the other
man's ear and asked if he would escort her to their room,
please, she found she wasn't feeling quite as well as she
thought after her bout with seasickness earlier. He rubbed
his arm and offered it to her for their trip to the
stateroom.

21

"I never knew a fan was a weapon before," he told her as they walked.

"I have several fans, each one has a different use. My Grandfather was always worried about someone kidnapping me for ransom, so I was taught in various means of self-defense. Suitable for a girl, of course."

"How did you get such an English name as Temperance?"

"My mother was English. My father met her while he was on a tour in Europe and they married before my Grandfather had a chance to separate them. By the time he found out, I was on my way. Then my mother died just after my youngest brother was born. Not from childbirth, she fell from a horse."

Charity caught up with them in the hallway just before they reached their room. They invited her in and she looked from one to the other of them like they were both crazy.

"I keep telling you two, you cannot socialize with me or even be seen talking to me without damaging your reputations. You two act like that is no big deal, but believe me, it is the most important thing you have and once it is damaged, nothing can give it back."

Temperance felt that Charity was speaking from experience but didn't want to embarrass her new friend by saying anything in front of Luke. Luke figured he knew what she was talking about and didn't want to embarrass his wife or Charity so he tipped his hat and bid them good evening, he thought he might join in the poker game setting up near the front deck on the ship and as the weather was quite nice, it should be a pleasant evening. Even if the ship was again beginning to roll a bit more in the waves. He hoped they hit the Inside Passage pretty soon. He never did care for sea travel.

Charity helped Temperance out of her evening dress and hung it up in the wardrobe. She wondered about the fancy men's riding pants and boots placed on top of one of the bags, but figured it really was none of her business.

They would be traveling up the Inside Passage soon, and no one would be suffering from seasickness then. It was like a ride on a smooth lake unless it was storming bad enough to make choppy whitecaps. But even then, it wasn't too bad unless you were in a small boat. Then, look out.

Temperance was asleep when Luke let himself in the room as it was nearing daylight. He had not planned on staying so late, but his luck at cards seemed incredible, so he kept playing, just one more hand.

She woke up as he was starting to undress and thought he was getting up. She smiled tentatively at him and he was afraid she would be repulsed by the smell of old cigars and whiskey that he was positive he reeked of, so kept his distance.

He grabbed a clean shirt from his wardrobe shelf and shrugged into it. "I'm going up for early breakfast. Do you want me to bring you anything?"

Just then the ship lurched into a series of wallows through the Straits of Juan de Fuca and her stomach lurched in time with the ship. He swore she turned green before his eyes. He had closed the window as soon as he entered the room, so the air was already starting to carry the scent of the engine room. When he closed his eyes, he started to get the same sick feeling. He rushed to the porthole and flung it open. A bit of spray hit him, but the rush of fresh air was wonderful.

"I don't care what they say, I'm leaving that open. Shall I help you over here for fresh air?" he asked.

She held still for a few moments, then reached for her wrapper to cover her voluminous nightgown which brought a small chuckle to her lips. The nightgown was one her old nurse had insisted all ladies wore to preserve their modesty. She was sure the sight of it would not incite her husband to passion and the wrapper over it was just one more huge layer between her and the world.

"Yes, I think fresh air would be wonderful. I thought I left the window open, it must have swung shut after I went to sleep. Charity told me that would help with my seasickness."

He felt bad about not admitting he was the one that closed it, then looked at her twinkling eyes and figured she already knew he did it. He chuckled weakly as he assisted her to the chair near the window. He knew there was a slender young woman somewhere under all those billows of material, but other than her hands and face, he sure couldn't see any sign of it.

He poured her a glass of water and set it near her on a small shelf with a rim around it to keep things from sliding off.

"If I see Charity, I will send her along to give you a hand," he told her as he left the room.

As soon as he was on deck, he settled into a chair and fell asleep. It had been a long night.

He slowly came awake to the sound of giggling somewhere nearby. He eased his hand up and raised his hat brim to see Temperance and Charity standing in the doorway, laughing to see him sleeping in the chair.

Charity still refused to come out and keep them company and muttered something about seeing if Doc had bothered seeing to the other girls.

"Other girls? There are more women on this ship?" Luke asked her.

"Yes sir. Doc has four young Oriental girls stashed down in the hold. He picked them up in San Francisco to put them to work in his business he wants to start in some new town starting up, in Alaska. Some place named Paradise. He figures it being a new town and all, he will get in on the ground floor and corner the market."

Luke was starting to get mad. He didn't even know this Doc character and already he didn't like him. Bringing girls that were virtually going to be his slaves to Luke's town. He didn't start his town to have it infected with scum. He excused himself and went in search of someone named Doc.

Chapter 3

By the time Luke found Doc, he had a slender idea of a plan. First he would offer to buy the girl's contracts. If that didn't work, he would throw Doc overboard.

Doc proved to be a scrawny, wheezy little man that he had seen often, sitting by himself in the back corner of the saloon deck. He was usually nursing a bottle of something and playing solitaire, shuffling badly and trying to practice sliding cards up his sleeve. Luke sat down across from him and told him if he got caught trying any of that in Paradise, he wouldn't have to worry about how to pay for his funeral, the town would supply it.

Doc seemed to shrivel down in his seat. Luke felt like a bully. Then he remembered the young women somewhere down in the hold. He grabbed Doc under an arm and hauled him to his feet.

"C'mon, we are going to take a little walk and discuss some property and values. Maybe we can make a deal," he told Doc.

They descended the stairs to the front hold and Luke felt his stomach start to heave. The air was dense with fumes and very little light filtered down this deep into the ship. Doc was fidgeting in his grasp but he never loosened it.

When they reached the stall the girls were kept in, he just about lost his lunch again. These were human beings being kept like animals in the hold with the horses and dogs. They were chained in the corners with some dirty straw on the floor, a bucket near each one for waste and another with a dipper for water to drink. Remnants of food lay in the dirty straw. Their hair was matted, their clothes filthy. The girls didn't look old enough to be away from their families.

"How much for their contracts?" Luke asked Doc.

"These here are my chance to make my fortune in Alaska. I'm setting up in a new town that has just been started by some stiff necked gold miner that don't know a thing about human nature or what real men need after working all week. I'm not selling."

"I hate to be the one to inform you, but that town belongs to me. If I see you anywhere within city limits, they will be burying you in the new cemetery I intend to establish just as soon as I get home. Now, how much do you want for their contracts? Maybe I should just toss you overboard and see how well you swim and wash some of the stench off you," he started for the stairs, still holding firmly to Doc's arm.

As they reached the top of the stairs, the Captain was just coming down.

"Is there a problem here?" he asked.

"No, Doc here was going to sell me his contracts for the four girls he has tethered in the hold," Luke told him.

"What? What girls? Doc, you told me you were transporting dogs to sell to the Miners. Let's go see about this."

They turned and back down the steps to the storage hold they went. Doc kept holding back and Luke figured his arm was going to be sore for quite a while from the grip Luke kept on it. When the Captain reached the stall the girls were kept in, Luke thought he was going to have apoplexy right then and there. If he had not had a good grip on Doc, the Captains' blow would have knocked him down. Doc slumped down and Luke was all that still held him up.

"Good Lord. What kind of man does something like this to other people? I don't know who we can ask to help these poor children out. I know their parents sell the girls on the streets in San Francisco, but I do not condone trafficking in humans," the Captain muttered.

"I offered to buy their contracts so he wasn't out the money. I thought we could clean them up and find jobs for them after we land," Luke told him.

"If they are let out on their own, someone just like Doc here, will grab them and they will be right back in the same line of work Doc planned for them."

They heard someone coming down the stairs and kept quiet until Charity rounded the end of the stall, carrying a tray of food and some towels. She was crooning and trying to reassure the girls that she was going to find a way to get them out of here when she ran into the Captain.

When she saw Luke and then Doc, she almost fainted. Then she straightened up and continued trying to wash the hands and faces of the girls. One of them was too ill to eat and the other three were only picking at the sandwiches she had filched from the lunch buffet on deck.

The Captain turned on her and started berating her for the current condition of the girls. She stood there in shock for a couple of minutes, then told him she had been tied down here at the beginning of the trip and he should check his load before leaving dock if he intended to get all high horse about it now.

He stopped in stunned surprise. "You were tied down here, too? How did you get loose and why are you down here now?"

"I convinced Doc that he was going to lose money on what he paid the man that brought me here if I died of seasickness on the way. He buys girls every time the ship docks. The man I thought was going to marry me, drugged me and sold me to him. I try to find enough food to bring down here and try to clean the poor things up a bit. They know what kind of life he has planned for them and one speaks some English. They are trying to die. I think the one might make it. She has not touched food or water since we left San Francisco. I can't rouse her."

Luke listened in growing horror. He realized he was a very sheltered young man. He had no idea there was a thriving slave trade going on in young women and so many years after the war over slavery and States Rights. He found out later slavery was only the excuse.

"Captain, is there an available cabin that we can take these young women to and see if we can rescue them?" Luke asked. "I will pay for the cabin."

"The fewer people know about their circumstances, the better chance they might have for some sort of better life in the future. You and I can move them up if there is a cabin fairly close to the stairs," he told Luke.

Charity told them there was a vacant cabin two doors down from the stairs. That was where she had been sleeping after everyone else turned in for the night. She had been keeping it clean so no one would notice.

Doc started mumbling about his investment. Luke rounded on him and told him he would repay a fair amount for the girl's contracts, but not to press his luck. He might get to swim for the closest island if he didn't shut up. Luke made him carry the sickest girl, while Charity helped the strongest one and he and the Captain each carried one of the other girls.

They were almost at the door to the cabin when the sick girl roused herself, saw who was carrying her and stuck a long slim knife under his ribs. She smiled, she had succeeded. As they fell to the floor, she breathed her last.

Charity thought that Temperance would like the chance to do something and forget her own miseries for a while, so she slipped away and brought a curious Temperance back with her. As soon as Temperance saw the condition of the girls, she started cleaning them up and planning what to dress them in. Charity figured if they could find Doc's room, they would find clothes. Not the kind

31

anyone should be seen in, but maybe something they could remake and use.

The Captain decided he wasn't needed, but did let them know where Doc had been staying. He and Luke went to Doc's room and found it stacked with trunks and cases of whiskey. The trunks were loaded with clothes and everything needed to start a saloon.

"I think Charity just got a new career and an inheritance, don't you?" Luke asked the Captain.

"I guess, if you are planning on taking care of those women, you might ask your wife about it though. Women get funny notions. I never figured you for putting little girls to work making that kind of living for you."

Luke almost hit him. "I plan on those little girls having a real life and Charity can sell all this and have enough to start a boarding house if she wants to. My wife needs a maid and if one of those girls is willing to learn, she can have a home with us. The way Temperance took over their care tells me I will probably be hiring the lot of them to keep our home and whatever else she decides for them."

The Captain was going to just have Doc and the dead girl sewn into one shroud for burial at sea, but Temperance told him he was not going to make that poor girl spend eternity clasped in her killers' arms. The Captain said it seemed more the other way around to him and Temperance told him that Doc had killed her just as surely as she had killed him. They had separate shrouds.

The service was short and they were consigned to the deep. The other passengers didn't even know what had happened and Luke figured it would be better that way.

Charity talked the cook into making a pot of rice and the girls finally ate. They were beautiful now that they were cleaned up and their hair was combed out.

Charity and Temperance started English lessons for them and they soon were speaking well enough to be understood, if Jasmine helped. She already knew some English and was a great help in teaching the other two. They had decided on names that everyone on board could pronounce. So now they were Jasmine, Pearl and Sue Lee as her real name was very close to that.

As it finally became clear that they would not have to live the life they were expecting when they were sold, they became happy chattering young women. Jasmine made the other two speak only in English, even when they were alone so they could find good work in the strange world they were going to, Alaska. The thought of what they might have to do if they didn't learn English was enough to make dedicated students out of them.

They were finally traveling through the Inside Passage and it was calm and beautiful. Everyone was enjoying the cruise. When Luke and Temperance even managed to make their marriage a real marriage, it was so relaxed and almost by accident that neither one had time to be nervous or scared.

Later, when Temperance said Thank You to Charity, Charity didn't have a clue what she was talking about. Then she saw the twinkle in Temperance's eyes and knew what she meant. They had a good laugh and became even better friends.

The morning Luke stepped back into their cabin, cleanly shaved, Temperance realized what a good looking husband she had. She kissed him on his smooth cheek and he decided he really liked being clean shaven.

As the ship crossed the Gulf of Alaska, they were back to rough seas and Temperance spent as much time as possible up on deck. It seemed to keep her from getting seasick.

When she first saw the snow peaks on the horizon, she thought they were strange clouds. She had never seen snow. The three young girls were joining her on deck most days and also thought they were seeing strange clouds. Charity, having grown up in Kansas was aware they were seeing some very large snow mountains even though she had never seen such mountains.

She tried to describe snow to four incredulous young women that thought surely she was teasing them. When Luke agreed with Charity, Temperance thought he was in on the joke.

"All right. I understand you like to joke around, but really, what you are telling me is unbelievable. I am supposed to believe those are very large mountains covered now in the middle of summer with frozen water?" Temperance frowned at him.

"It's snow. We have snow up here over half of the year. You will see more of it than you ever imagined," he told her.

She silently wondered just what she had let herself in for, although she really hadn't had any say in whether or not she would marry. Evidently people survived in those conditions, but she was certainly unprepared.

The day the ship started up the wide canal from the Gulf of Alaska to the community of Valdez, she was enthralled by the beauty of the green hills around her and the snow covered mountains just beyond the green. She saw white mt. goats on craggy bluffs looking out over the channel. They spotted a black bear on the edge of the water, intently watching the small stream that entered the ocean there. She was delighted to see it scoop up a large fish and take off back into the trees with it. Then a very large brown colored bear sauntered over to the same location and took up watching the water. It too soon scooped up a large fish and stayed right where it was to eat it. The only thing that would make it move away was the desire to nap or a larger bear.

Valdez was a bustling small town and the ship docked amid much noise and activity on the part of the people on the dock. It was named in 1790, with a town being built as part of a scam to lure gold seekers away from the Klondike in 1898. With the summer road called the Richardson Trail being built in 1899 it finally had access to the rest of Alaska. Being an ice free Port helped.

Luke escorted her down the gangplank which was actually a set of movable stairs to the dock itself. He had already arranged to have their luggage and other cargo taken to their rooms at the hotel. Charity and the three girls would possibly already be there by the time they finished looking at every single new thing that caught her eye.

There were men of all nationalities helping unload the ship and she had never seen so many races represented. The women waiting up on the shore for some of the men getting off the ship surprised her even more. Most were local women and very nice looking. None were dressed as she was. Wanting to make a good impression, she was dressed in one of her finest walking dresses with a fur trimmed pelisse and hat. Since her hands had been cold, she was carrying a small muff. The other women looked at her in awe.

None of them had ever seen such a sight. A good portion of the men stopped and looked at her, also. She looked so delicate that a good breeze might carry her away. Never in the history of Valdez had so much elegance graced their shore.

Luke wasn't sure whether or not he should be proud of how beautiful she looked or mad at how greedy the other men looked, that were staring at her. He was saved from having to pound some sense or manners into them by the foreman yelling at them to get to work, they weren't being paid to gawk.

Temperance's cheeks were bright pink and he couldn't tell if it was from the chill wind from the sea and surrounding snow mountains or from embarrassment.

As they entered the hotel, a dapper gentleman dressed almost in the male equivalence of Temperance's outfit doffed his hat to her and almost fell down the few steps to the street. The smell of alcohol was quite strong on his trail and they both refused to acknowledge him.

The person manning the front desk about fell over his own feet trying to get the doors and escorting them to their rooms. He assured them that dinner would be served promptly at 6 p.m. They would want to be among the first ones in the dining room as sometimes the cook didn't prepare exactly enough of each item. Like a good portion of the local population, he had a bit of a drinking problem although he didn't consider it a problem unless there wasn't enough.

Chapter 4

The room was not very large. They had taken two rooms that joined if the doors were opened between them. Even with both rooms joined, the space available was going to be very tight once all the trunks, boxes and other women arrived. Temperance asked Luke if he thought maybe they ought to take another room, also. If he didn't mind, that is.

Luke reached the lobby just as Charity ushered in the three girls. From the crowd outside, it looked like half the dock workers had followed them here. He asked Charity if they were okay and she said if they were still in Doc's line of business, they would have just made a fortune. She hoped they had sturdy doors and good locks in this hotel.

The clerk assured her they had the best and Luke secured two more rooms beside theirs. He asked about bathes for all the women and the clerk was still trying to figure out the logistics when Luke escorted the women up to their rooms. For sure, they could not use the public bathes down the street.

Temperance and Charity had made some acceptable clothing from the outfits they found in the trunks in Doc's room for the young women and now they were dressed in style, even if the fabrics were very bright. The colors suited the girls though and they looked very lovely.

Temperance was changed into her evening dress to go down to dinner after she finished her bath. The hot water had felt wonderful. Luke wasn't sure what the locals were going to make of his lovely elegant wife. He doubted anyone ever dressed up just to eat, here.

Charity and the girls were ready to eat, also, so they made a grand procession as they descended the stairs and entered the dining room. The girls were dressed in jewel tones of satin, Charity wore a deep burgundy gown she had managed to add enough ruffles and lace to, to make it decent to wear in public. The oriental girls thought the small bustles were hilarious and once she looked at it from their perspective, she figured they actually were. However on Temperance, the style looked stunning. The rest of them would live with it.

Dinner was served to their table in family style. Platters and bowls brought out from the kitchen and placed in the center of the table and help yourself. The oriental girls were still looking for the rice when Charity filled their plates and told them to just eat, she doubted there would be any rice.

Luke made a mental note to try to find some bags of rice to take home with them. He doubted if there was much rice in his supplies at the house, either.

All the women were still waiting for it to get dark when Luke told them they really needed to get some rest as tomorrow they needed to start packing for the trip on home. They were all incredulous when he told them it would only be a few hours of not quite dark here on the coast but where they were going, there would not be any darkness until late August. He said they would be traveling by wagon tomorrow and it would take them over a week to reach home, probably closer to two weeks, even if everything went well.

Temperance asked if he were going to ride in one of the wagons and he told her he would ride a horse. She asked if she could ride a horse also, as she was a good rider. He was stumped as to where he would find not only a gentle dependable horse but a sidesaddle in Valdez. Even if he could, would any horse here accept the fluttering skirts and strangeness of a sidesaddle? He needn't have worried.

When he came up to the room to tell Temperance they were ready to leave, she met him at the door in her riders' pants with the flared bottoms and boots, her jacket form fitting in the best gaucho manner. The stock whip coiled over her shoulder and her Spanish style riding hat on her head. She looked stunning but he wasn't sure if Valdez was ready for the sight of a woman wearing tight pants and boots. She threw a small cape over her shoulder and it did cover most of her.

When they stepped into the street, she looked at the horses and walked directly to the one that was prancing around on his lead and misbehaving. She sprung lightly up onto his back, grabbed the reins from the young man holding him and trotted him to the end of the street, then loosened the reins and kicked his ribs, letting him race up the side of the steep hill. He was more subdued as he carefully picked his way back down and settled down for the rest of the day.

Luke rode the placid old mare back to the stable and traded her in on a more lively horse. So much for his delicate wife not being able to handle the ride.

Travel from Valdez to the interior of the Territory was over very rough ground and the road was not what most people would have considered a road. It carried the name of the Richardson Trail/Highway, but it barely consisted of a series of ruts. Since it was all there was, they made do. The extra team of horses the stable had insisted on now made sense. When they bogged down, the spare team pulled them out.

The first couple of days they did not make very good time and Luke revised his estimate of how long it would take them to reach Paradise.

However, once they were over the range of mountains near the coast, they made far better time. Temperance did not carry the whip just for show. She could encourage a reluctant horse to pick up the pace and her mount soon learned not to flinch or shy when the whip whistled past his head. She was not cruel with it, but she could flick a fly off a horse's rump without touching the horse.

When one of the hired drovers attempted to grab one of the girls, he found she could also raise the hide on a man's backside with it, and he didn't want to know exactly how hard she could hit with it. All the men were very respectful after that, to all the women.

The scenery was breathtaking. Lower elevations were all shades of green with the stark mountains rearing up behind the lower foothills. There were waterfalls everywhere from snow melt higher up. Glaciers slowly ground their way through valleys they were grinding wider and deeper. Where some were receding, glacial moraines littered the landscape.

Her first moose left her wondering, just why was the animal so clumsy looking, yet moved with swift grace through the boggy tundra? She wondered whether or not one could be broke to ride? They would fare much better traveling through this terrain than the poor horses.

When they came over one rise and saw hundreds of caribou spread out over the huge valley below them, she thought of home. This time of year, the caribou were not bunched in large herds, but they were starting to congregate in the same areas towards migration and rut later in the autumn. They reminded her of her Grandfathers huge herds of cattle, loosely ranging in the hills and valleys on the ranch.

"Luke? Is Paradise much like this land? All green and rugged mountains?" she asked.

"It has the greens and lots of hills, not quite the same mountains although you can see even bigger mountains but they are quite a ways away from town. I think it is all nice, but I might be a bit prejudiced about it," he answered.

"Describe it to me, Luke," she asked.

"I think it is very nice. I placed the town on the hills at the head of the valley, just beside the reservoir. The valley has the gold so there wasn't much reason to place the town where it would just get dug up. There is a ditch that brings water from the reservoir around the hill to town. So far, the water level has never dropped low enough to require hauling water in. There are some trees along the streets, but not as many as I would have liked to have left."

"It sounds like you planned it very well, Luke. I will be happy to reach Paradise. Why did you name it that?"

"Uh, it's a pretty place, Temperance. I better go help the drovers through this next stretch of road. It might be boggy," and he rode away. What had he been thinking, to name his town after a house of ill repute that he had fond memories of? No way could he ever explain THAT to his lady wife.

Temperance knew a dodge when she heard one. Now she was curious.

She rode by the wagon that Charity and the three girls were riding on, for a while. She was deep in thought when Charity finally tossed a branch at her and her horse shied.

"Oops, sorry, just trying to get your attention. What are you thinking so hard about?" Charity asked her.

"Sorry, I was trying to figure out a way to learn how the town of Paradise got its' name. Luke acted oddly when I asked him. Now it is nagging at me."

"Off the subject, but how are things going for you and Luke?" Charity asked her.

"I think everything is going very well. He even shaved those whiskers. So far, he is very good to me. I just don't know what to expect once we reach his town of Paradise." Temperance replied.

"None of us do, Temperance, it is going to be a surprise for all of us. I'm not even sure he knows what he wants, either."

Charity was right about that. The closer they got to Paradise, the more Luke wondered just what he had been thinking to head outside, intent on getting a high class wife and dragging her back here to the backside of beyond. He didn't even know if his house would be completed by the time they arrived. The furniture he had ordered and sent on ahead to be delivered while he was gone, should already be in place. He certainly hoped it was.

Now he was worried the women would all freeze to death this coming winter. A lady from southern California wouldn't be as used to cold weather as a lady from Seattle. She didn't even know what snow looked like and certainly had never touched any. He would have to see if he could find a local lady to help outfit her and the other women also.

He left to find a wife and not only returned with a fancy wife but three Celestials and a possibly ex-lady of ill repute. This wasn't quit what he had in mind when he left here.

Somehow, most of Doc's stock for a saloon managed to still be in his possession, also. No one in Valdez had the money to buy it. For a man that seldom had a drink, he was going to have the best stocked supply of whiskey in the entire Territory. The gaudy decorations didn't suit his ideas for his home, either.

As they approached the hills surrounding Paradise, Luke found that his hands were sweaty and he didn't feel so good. Now that they were within a day or two of ending their trip, he wanted to just keep going. The trip was pleasant and the weather had held off on rain. The voracious bug population was slowed from the horrendous early summer mosquitoes and no rain meant the next wave of blood suckers had yet to hatch.

Maybe they could just wander around in the Wilderness like Moses did. 40 years seemed about right. Maybe he would know what to do by then.

Temperance wondered why they seemed to have slowed the pace they were traveling down to a crawl. She could walk faster than they were progressing, with Luke stopping the entire procession to check a squeaky axle or to see if the women were in need of a break every few minutes.

When they stopped for their midday meal, they could still see where last night's camp had been, farther down the valley.

"Luke, what is wrong?" she asked him when they had a few moments alone.

"Wrong? Nothing's wrong," he grumped.

"Then why are we making worse time on the best part of the entire trail we have been on since we left Valdez?"

"I hadn't noticed the trail being all that good anywhere. I should have taken a house in Valdez and waited out the winter there and brought you out here next summer. I just hope construction is finished on our house."

"Luke, we have been camping since we left Valdez, if the house isn't finished, we can camp out some more. It won't be a problem."

Luke hoped that was true. He didn't have a good feeling about what he was going to find when they topped the next hill and could actually see the town. He had been so proud of it when he left, but after seeing the towns in Washington and California, he felt inadequate. What did he really know about laying out a town? He wanted something that would last, even after the gold ran out.

As they started down the long sweeping curve of the trail into the valley, they could see men working at intervals along the creek. They were busy shoveling dirt into long wooden sluice boxes and once in a while, one would straighten up and see them, then wave. They never paused for very long. Mining season was very short and until they cleaned up the box, they would not know if they were working in vain or if they were even making wages, let alone making a fortune.

Ditches brought water farther up on the sides of the valley into the edges of the hills and more sluice boxes ran down from these ditches with even more men shoveling dirt into them. It all reminded Temperance of an ant hill. Most of the men lived in tents near their sluice boxes but quite a few would head for town as soon as they quit shoveling for the day.

Charity looked the town over thoroughly as they proceeded through it. The streets were laid out wide enough to park wagons in front of businesses. There were a few trees left here and there but they looked rather forlorn with none close by. There were a few businesses and the busiest was the café. It was still mostly tent, but there was some construction going on over and around it.

47

The long trestle tables inside were clean and the benches beside them looked fairly splinter free. The tables were already set for the evening meal.

Now that she was here, she wondered just what she was going to do. She really did not want to start up the line of work Doc had planned for her and the other girls. She would rather marry the first man that asked her and at least be a respectable woman.

Luke had the wagons stop at the café and stepped in to see about getting a meal before they started up to the house. He didn't want to have a lack of a kitchen looming over them if the house was not finished.

The cook was an older man that was unable to work the long grueling hours required for mining and decided he would mine the Miners by supplying them meals. He offered to fix sandwiches right away or if they could wait a little bit, he could have a full meal ready for them. After seeing that the plates were nailed to the tables, Luke thought maybe sandwiches would be fine.

They did not question what the meat in the sandwiches used to be. It was tender and tasted good. The bread was the ever present sourdough. Everyone thanked the cook and they continued on their way.

Chapter 5

As they reached the end of the street, they saw a lovely house. The yard was all dirt yet but there were a couple of spruce trees on one side and a cluster of birch on the other side so the house looked like it had been there a while but was still being finished. There was none of the gingerbread trim so beloved of the bigger homes in Seattle and most of the ones in San Francisco. This house looked like it would be first and foremost, a home without pretensions of grandeur. Temperance liked it immediately. Luke groaned that they had not fancied it up.

"Why do you want it to look differently, Luke? Will doodads make it more comfortable or warmer? I like it just as it is." Temperance told him.

"You're just saying that to make me feel better," he said.

"Luke. I never say something just because it might make someone feel better. Then they only feel worse when they find out the truth. Why would I lie? If you think I am a liar, then you have not been paying attention," she kicked her horse into a gallop and headed for the house.

Charity snickered, "She should have been a redhead."

Luke's ears were red and he kept his face turned away as they started toward the house again. He could see his wife walking up to the front door and opening it. Wasn't he supposed to carry her over the threshold or something?

Temperance peeked inside the house but did not go in. She closed the door and walked around to the side of the house, looking it all over from the outside. It was a nice size and would be even better once they planted some shrubs and flowers around the outside to make it look lived in.

She walked back around the house and met Luke as he came up the walkway to the porch. She placed her gloved hand on his arm and turned to walk with him. She was not even too surprised when he swept her up in his arms to walk into the house, then stood there wondering how he was going to open the door. She reached down and turned the knob.

"That is how we will build our lives, Luke. Helping each other and cooperation. You carry the loads, I will open the doors."

The inside of the house was still being worked on. They could hear banging upstairs and in the back of the house. Luke continued carrying her into the back to see what the noise was about. She stopped him after a few steps and told him to put her down, she could walk. He surprised her by kissing her while he still held her. Then he gently lowered her feet to the floor.

The rooms they passed through were well proportioned and she could see how it could become a very fine home indeed. When they reached the kitchen, she immediately

51

saw what the noise was all about. Four men were trying to bring a huge wood cookstove in through a doorway that was just a bit too narrow.

"Luke, why not have then remove the door frame and it should come right in," she whispered.

Luke yelled over the noise the men were making, "Hey, my wife says to remove the door frame."

The men stopped, looked at them, looked at the door frame and each other and started laughing. "Why didn't one of us professionals notice that?"

One grabbed a pry bar and they soon had the frame removed and the stove in place. Tacking the frame back in position was a simple matter and they proceeded to install the chimney. There was a wood heater beside it that the men called a trash burner.

A large enameled sink was along one wall with plenty of work surface on both sides of it. A pitcher pump supplied water to the sink with a pitcher of water beside it to prime the pump with. A cool box was built into the north wall with screen over the exterior to keep flies out of the food to be stored in it. There was a large U shaped pantry in the center of the house with two doors entering it from the kitchen for ease of filling and finding supplies stored in it. The dining room was still unfinished but had a china hutch built into one wall. She could picture her china and silver placed in it, from some of her trunks.

The formal parlor would take more time to furnish and to her, it was not a priority. There was a powder room for guests near the parlor.

The library was in the final stages of having book shelves built along all the interior walls. The family parlor was taking shape nicely and she thought it was the most welcoming room in the house. It had a large wood burning heater in it and she hoped the warmth would reach other parts of the house if it was as cold here as Luke told her it was for most of the year. Luke said there would be wood heaters in a few of the other rooms also, but this and the kitchen stoves would be the main ones kept going all the time.

Eventually there would be a fancy parlor stove in the formal parlor.

They went up the stairs side by side. When they reached the top, Luke wasn't as sure of what each room was as it had not been finished when he left. They opened doors and explored and she fell in love with the large room over the front of the house. She could see almost the entire town from the bow window seat. Even with no cushion on it, it was a comfortable place to sit.

There was a smaller room beside it that Luke said was for her trunks and clothes, if she liked it. The wardrobes would be built later for most storage and clothing.

There was a powder room next to their bedroom and several other bedrooms along the central hallway. It was going to be a grand house. To think it was being built out in the middle of Alaska was unbelievable. No one had a house like this up here. Luke told her the walls were all filled with sawdust to help keep the house warmer in the winter. They were also twice as thick as the usual home. He wanted it to be comfortable.

Charity was looking over the kitchen and decided she would not mind cooking in a place like this. Maybe Luke would hire her for a while, until she found a job. She had been doing most of the cooking on the trail north. The three young women trailed along behind her. They were so forlorn and lost looking she decided she better talk to Luke and Temperance soon to see just what they were expected to do.

As far as they knew, since Doc had bought them from their parents, he owned them and Luke was now their owner, even though he wasn't the one that killed Doc. They just could not accept the idea that no one owned them.

Luke asked the men working on the house if any of the furniture had been delivered yet. Then found that indeed it had been, but they didn't know where to put it, so everything was stored behind the house with a roof over it. They thought the shed would be a good woodshed once the furniture was out of it.

Temperance came outside and asked about setting up beds in the rooms they would be using, first. Once they reached the shed, they decided maybe it would be easier to start moving furniture indoors just to reach the items they needed that appeared to be at the back.

Luke asked the men working on finishing up trim around windows and doors if they knew anyone that would be willing to come help move furniture into the house. They said they would help as the rest of their crew and the only ones available seemed to have found a supply of whiskey and were in no condition to handle nice belongings.

Luke ran to the second wagon in the ones they had just arrived in and sure enough, someone had opened a crate holding bottles of whiskey and several bottles were missing. Then he heard singing and followed it to the banks of the creek where he found his three wagon drivers sprawled on the bank with four other men, each drinking from their own bottle and all too drunk to stand.

Luke worked his way down the bank, smashing bottles and throwing drunks into the icy waters of the creek. He heard a scream behind him and saw a man holding his wrist and his wife holding her whip. The man started searching the creek for the gun he had dropped when the whip snaked around his hand.

As he bent over, the whip flicked his rump and he screeched again.

"You will not act like a coward and try to shoot anyone in the back. You will now walk out of the water and forget about your gun," She told the man.

He came out of the water, holding his wrist and rubbing his rump. He made a grab for her as he reached the bank and she kicked him in the face, whirled and kicked him back into the creek on his backside. By this time, Luke reached him and lifted him by the scruff of his neck and pitched him out on the bank.

"What is your name?" he asked the man.

"Josh Wilcox, what's it to ya?" he snarled.

"Well, I just like to know the name of anyone in the area that has a tendency to try shooting anyone in the back.

You stole whiskey from my wagon and yet you act the abused person. What are you doing on my property, anyway?" Luke told him.

"Your property? This place belongs to some stiff necked old geezer that don't appreciate the house we are building or fine whiskey, either," Josh said.

"I may not be the youngest man in town, but make no mistake, I own this property and this house and that wagon load of whiskey. Again, what are you doing here?"

"I'm working on this elephant of a house. Everyone knows it is too big for this climate and whoever lives in it is going to freeze to death this winter. So if that is you and this snooty dame with the whip, enjoy it."

"You DID work on this house, you are no longer employed. I'll tell the foreman and he will pay you up to date, minus the cost of the bottle of whiskey."

"Ha. I am the foreman."

"Maybe you were the foreman a few hours ago, you are no longer. The man that was seeing to the stove and chimney installation has just been promoted." Luke turned, offered his arm to Temperance and walked back to the house.

"Thank you for saving me a hole in my hide back there. I know you said your Grandfather had you learn self-defense but that was amazing."

"Grandfather didn't have me learn any of that. The whip I learned working cattle and horses. The kicks I learned from Sue Lee. She has many talents."

When he reached the house, he saw the man he just promoted put a rifle back down by the door and start working again.

He sent Temperance upstairs to decide which rooms would be assigned to which woman and went back to find the men working on the house.

"Thanks for covering my back when Josh became a problem. Between you and my wife, I was well protected. You are now the foreman of this job and how much pay is owed to Josh and the others?"

"Your friend that is running the assay office in town has kept us paid up to date. Josh and the others only get today's pay to be current. I will try to finish up the job as fast as we can, sir. We've been working short shifts since you left or the place would have been finished by now."

Luke mulled this over as he figured out the pay due each man. Then he spotted his friend walking up the hill to the house. When Mitch reached the porch, Luke opened the door and they shook hands and pounded each other on the back a while. Then he told Mitch he fired Josh and the three men with him that were slowly walking over to receive their pay, minus the price of a bottle of whiskey each.

He also told him he had promoted the man coming in the room from the back of the house. Mitch introduced him to Luke as Gary OldMan.

"We will have supper then be back to help put furniture in the house," he told Luke.

As soon as the crew were paid off and left, Mitch turned to Luke, "Did you find her? The woman you've been planning on for as long as I have known you? Is she here?"

He heard sounds upstairs and then the five women came to the head of the stairs and started down.

"Good Lord Almighty. You couldn't make up your mind so you brought a harem?" Mitch exclaimed.

Luke blushed beet red. Temperance had heard most of the exchange and she smiled at Mitch.

"Allow me to introduce Luke's harem. This is Charity, this one is Pearl, this is Jasmine and this is Sue Lee. I am Temperance."

The five women lined up in front of Mitch and each one smiled sweetly at Luke.

Mitch saw the look on Luke's face and started laughing. Luke blushed even more and started to say something, then stopped and started yet again, but could only sputter.

"What is the matter, Husband? Did you swallow something the wrong way?" Temperance asked him, smiling all the while.

Charity could barely contain her giggles and soon the other three were giggling also. Temperance managed to still look slightly serious.

"You explain it to him, Temperance," Luke managed to say. "Mitch, this is my wife, Temperance. Temperance, this is my best friend, Mitch."

Chapter 6

Temperance smiled at Mitch and reached out her hand to shake. Mitch was dazzled by her smile. Her hand felt small but her grip was firm and her hand did not feel soft like a pampered woman's hand usually did. It felt capable.

He noticed something coiled around over her shoulder but didn't want to appear snoopy so didn't say anything. Later he learned from gossip around town that it was a whip and she had used it on Josh Wilcox who considered himself a dangerous man.

He still didn't know why Luke had all these extra women in his house. They were all pretty women and he really liked looking at them. Maybe Luke had the right idea. Find a wife and get married.

While they were still talking, the crew returned to bring in furniture, Luke and Mitch pitched in and Temperance was busy directing where she wanted each piece place. Once the beds were found, the other women busied themselves making beds for the night. Everyone was worn out by the time most of the furniture was in the house as the beds were far in the back of the shed. At least it was light all night so they were not working in the dark. However, by the time they were finished, they were all famished.

Charity fired up the big stove in the kitchen. Jasmine and Sue Lee brought in supplies from the wagon and they all started a meal. Luke thought maybe the remaining whiskey should be brought in or the rest might be gone by morning if word was traveling around town and the camps as fast as it usually did.

He and Mitch unloaded most of the wagon and brought everything into the house, then packed most of it upstairs into one of the empty rooms.

At present, most of the rooms were still unpainted plaster over cloth bonded to the walls. Luke wanted to leave the colors and whether to paint or wallpaper the walls to his wife. Temperance liked it the way it was. It reminded her of home. She would add color with the curtains, pillows and artwork.

After they all finished eating, Mitch checked his watch and told them it was after midnight. Temperance found it hard to believe. It was still as bright as any time during the day. The sun was just behind a hill to the north, but it would soon be showing on the other side.

Mitch left, Luke locked the doors and they all went to bed. No one moved until they were awakened by a loud banging on the door.

Luke dressed hurriedly and made it to the door before whomever thought whatever they wanted to say was so important that they would actually damage the door.

He heard the window open above his head as he opened the door and saw a rifle barrel poke out a small space.

The red faced man standing at the door was too angry to stop and think before he took a swing at Luke. The shot above his head sobered him up quite a bit.

Luke had ducked the swing and now stood looking at the man standing in front of him.

"And just what do I owe the pleasure of this visit to?" he asked the man.

"Where is my whiskey and the women I sent Doc to buy?"

"Such a pleasant day and I don't believe I caught your name in the middle of that swing you aimed at my head. Do you want to start over and tell me why you think you are going to traffic in slavery in my town?"

"Slavery? Who said anything about slavery? I just want what I paid for."

"When you buy a human that is called slavery. Slavery was abolished. Therefore, you don't really want to be standing there telling me you bought some people."

"B-b-but, I paid out good money. You have to give them to me."

"No, I don't have to give you anything. If you can prove you paid Doc for the whiskey, I will let you repay me for the freight of bringing it here, and then you can move it right on out of town. But there is no way you are taking people as though they were animals."

"He was supposed to buy some of the Celestials spare girls. They aren't really people."

Charity and the girls were dressed by now and standing in the room behind Luke. He opened the door and pointed to them. "You mean to stand there and tell me those lovely women are not human? If you consider them animals, are you planning on some new way to pander to the tastes of degenerates?"

The man looked at the lovely women standing there dressed in current fashions, with their hair piled in fashionable curls on their heads. Their skin a pale smooth ivory.

"Those aren't what I bought. I bought the yellow girls they sell in China town. What are you trying to do, get me in trouble? That there redhead is no saloon worker, either, so you just prance out my girls and send these back."

Temperance made an entrance then, gliding down the stairs in the best grand lady manner. The man at the door about swallowed his tongue then stuttered when he looked at her.

"Luke, we need to advertise for more help around here. I don't think the five of us women can manage everything that needs done around the house. We should have accepted the others for more help instead of leaving them in Valdez."

"Valdez? You left people in Valdez?" the man asked.

"Not really. There were just several offers of help and we turned them all down," she replied. "I believe Charity, Sue, Pearl and Jas will be able to manage the house, but we need yard people and someone to handle the horses and cut firewood."

63

The man wasn't certain, but he felt he had missed something there. It was obvious there were no women here to work in his saloon he planned on building. He had figured to make the girls work out of one of the empty tents he had found until they earned enough to build a fancy saloon. They would be unsuitable by then to work in it, so he would just buy some more. They could do the cleaning and whatever other duties would be required. Now he was stumped.

He didn't have enough money to pay the man for freighting the whisky and he didn't have any women to work for him, either. Doc actually had used mostly his own money for the purchase of the whiskey and girls but he wasn't ever going to tell anyone that.

As he stomped away, Gary OldMan came up the track to the house.

"Say, what was Reggie Morse doing here? He sure didn't look happy when he left," Gary said.

"The man expected us to hand over the women and the whiskey so he could start a saloon. Seems he had a deal with Doc to buy some girls outside and figured these are the ones he was expecting. Just whereabouts in town did he expect to be able to start that kind of business?" Luke asked.

Gary scratched his chin and thought a bit, then told Luke he might have expected to buy out the lady that had a laundry down near the creek. She had injured her back and was having a time trying to stay in business.

Charity perked up at the mention of a business and stepped over to the men. "Maybe I could go talk to her and offer her a deal. I need work and she needs help."

Temperance came over and told her she didn't have to find work that was so hard, she could stay with them.

Charity told her that even though her name was Charity, she wasn't planning on living on theirs and this was her chance to make an honest living. If possible, she would like to rent her room from them, though. They continued talking about it through breakfast.

Temperance knew when to draw back and regroup. She instead offered to go down to the Laundry with Charity and see the town while they were at it. She really had not paid any attention on her way through it yesterday.

The other three women knew what Reggie wanted from them and decided they would rather stay in the house for now. Was there anything they could do around the house?

Temperance was still thinking when Charity asked if they would mind unpacking the trunks in Temperance's room and arranging everything in the small room beside it. There were plenty of shelves and they could hang the fancy dresses up to start losing some of the wrinkles.

Temperance wasn't positive that was a good idea, but then decided not to say anything as the girls were happy to have something to do.

She and Charity started down the walk and Luke soon caught up with them.

"I'm not certain that it is a very good idea for you two to walk unescorted through town after the visit from Reggie this morning. I don't know the man, but he was not in the mood to listen or to take his perceived loss lightly."

"If he really did give a lot of money to Doc, maybe he does own the whiskey, anyway. However, he still needs to show some sort of proof. He didn't look affluent enough to be investing a lot of cash," Charity said.

"That's what I was thinking. I want to talk to Mitch about him and see what he thinks," Luke told them.

When the walked past the Assay Office, Luke pointed just ahead to the sign that said Laundry and told them to either meet him here at Mitch's or he would meet them at the Laundry, depending on who finished first. He excused himself and walked across the street to the Assay Office and went inside.

Temperance and Charity walked into the large Laundry tent. An older woman was feeding a large fire under a huge vat of clothes, then picked up a funnel shaped metal plunger with vents cut in the sides on a wooden handle and began working the clothes with the plunger. Her face reflected the pain she was feeling and she stopped as soon as she spotted the two young women stepping through the flap in the tent.

"How may I help you ladies? I didn't realize there were any other women here yet. It's been a chore setting up a respectable business and hard to find anyone to build me a good sized building to house this Laundry before winter sets in. The only reliable carpenter has been working on a house for the owner of the town. The rest all say they will do the job, but just as soon as they hear about someone finding another streak of gold on a bench or in the creek, they are gone. I'm Mattie Davis," she held out her damp hand, then wiped it on her apron and held it out again.

Charity stepped up and spoke, "I'm Charity Canfield and I have a proposition for you."

At the horrified look on the older woman's face, Charity figured she should reword that.

"Not an indecent one. I want to either go into business with you or go to work for you. I would like to work towards part ownership at some date, instead of wages, if possible."

Mattie relaxed and told them as the only woman in town, she had gotten some very interesting "offers" from many of the men in the area. She said they didn't even care that she was old enough to be Mother to most of them.

Even some weasel named Reginald Morse had made an indecent proposal just a few days ago. She had smacked him with her plunger and now it had a dent in one side. She had met his partner, Doc, before Doc left and he was the brains and money behind the whole idea and that wasn't saying a whole lot about either of them as neither had a brain between them.

She had flat told them NO, but then she somehow managed to slip where she knew there was no mud only a few minutes earlier and then they renewed their offer to buy her out. She didn't like either one of them and she disapproved of the business they wanted to use the lot for so continued to tell them No. Things kept disappearing or turning up broken and she was sure it was Reggie's doing.

While they were talking, they heard a sound out behind the tent and Temperance pulled back her small cape and unslung the whip from over her shoulder. She stepped to the back tent flap and opened it quickly in time to see Reggie pouring something around the bottom of the tent and the scent of coal oil hit her. She snapped the whip and took off a patch of skin then another and another.

Reggie was dancing around in agony, screaming his head off and Temperance continued to skin him a small patch at a time. His back and neck were bleeding quite freely by the time Luke raced around the side of the tent in time to see his delicate little wife take off another patch of flesh.

"Uh, Temperance, maybe that is enough at present. If he hasn't seen the error of his ways, by now, then you can continue teaching him lessons."

Temperance coiled up her whip, placed it back over her shoulder and pulled her cape over it. She, Charity and Mattie started trying to clean the coal oil away from the tent. Just one careless match could send the entire business up in smoke. Luke grabbed Reggie by a place on his arm that wasn't bloody and told him since he poured the oil, he could help clean it up. He was sobbing in pain, but Temperance caressed the handle of her whip and he jumped right into pouring hot soapy water over the coal oil soaked ground and tent canvas.

Chapter 7

By the time they had most of the oil cleaned away from the tent, there were several other willing workers lending a hand. This was the only Laundry in town and no one wanted Mattie to close up or quit or lose her business.

The man setting up shop as a doctor stopped by and offered to patch up Reggie after he finished his current job. Mattie asked Temperance if she could teach her how to handle a whip like that. Temperance told her she wasn't sure she could teach it, she had been using a whip since she was a small child, first the short whip, then the current stock whip.

Mattie asked Charity how soon she could start and they returned to the vat of clothes, to wring them as dry as possible and hang them to dry. Temperance walked across the street with Luke to Mitch's office.

Shortly after Luke and Temperance walked downtown, the other three women were struggling to bring in barrels from the last wagon when the crew came around the corner and jumped in to assist them. Gary asked why they didn't tell the men what to do and Jasmine smiled shyly at him and said, "We didn't want to disturb you. You have a job to do, so do we."

"I don't think they expected you ladies to move these big barrels. They weigh more than any two of you put together. Dave, Joe, see about bringing in the rest of the barrels and supplies out of the wagon. The ladies can tell you where to set them down, in the house."

Dave and Joe hurried to comply as they wanted to look good in the eyes of the prettiest women they had ever seen. The girls blushed and kept their heads down and their eyes hidden.

Luke and Temperance returned home a short while later and by the time Charity returned home that evening, she was very tired but exhilarated to be a new partner in a Laundry. Mitch had walked her home.

Mitch was fascinated by this pretty girl that talked so tough and wasn't afraid of some hard work, yet was kind to Mattie and helped even before she knew whether or not Mattie would accept her offer to work in exchange for a partnership.

They were pleasantly surprised to find that supper was ready for them. Mitch was invited to join them and they enjoyed the meal Pearl had prepared.

As they walked through the house, they saw the three women had been very busy indeed. Colorful throws and pillows decorated chairs and settees. Some lovely paintings leaned against walls in various rooms where the girls thought they would look good but they didn't want to pound in nails or hang them without approval.

The china hutch in the dining room now held all her china and silverware. A lace runner covered the top of the bottom cabinets and candelabras placed at intervals on top the runner added more elegance to the room. The huge table was still pushed against an outside wall, but now a lace tablecloth graced it with more candelabras down the middle with a large silver bowl set in the middle holding some wildflowers placed in a glass container in the bowl. The effect was lovely if unusual.

The house was being transformed into a home. There were still curtains to be hung and the heavy drapes would help keep out drafts in colder weather.

The wagons' contents were now dispersed throughout the kitchen with a large pile remaining in the center of the floor. All the pots, pans and baking pans were now on shelves, hung from hooks or pegs. Canisters and bowls were lined up on the work surfaces around the room and the sturdy work table was still piled high with assorted supplies. The huge barrels lined up against one wall got Luke's attention.

"How the devil did you move those barrels? I would have got some men to come help with those and I'm sorry I forgot all about them. Are you all okay?"

Jasmine reassured him they had only moved one barrel and the crew brought in the rest. She didn't know where to put them, so they just had them placed back a bit out of the way.

When Charity saw them there, she thought that would make them handier to use than placed back in the dark pantry. Since they were full of flour, beans, oatmeal, cornmeal and cones of sugar, she didn't think they would need to be moved. In fact, the barrel of molasses would be easier to use from if it were not too cold and it happened to be closer to the stoves so would stay fluid.

The smaller barrels of pickles were placed back in the pantry until Gary came in and showed them the trapdoor that led to a small cellar under the house. Then the small pickle barrels were moved down to the cellar to keep them cool and crisp. The crocks of jam, butter, lard and cured meats were placed down there also. Sides of bacon were hung down in the cellar with some cured smoked hams. The room was just above freezing and would remain at that temperature all year around.

When Gary came to work the next morning, he had a small bucket full of wild blueberries he had just picked. He told Charity where they were located and how to preserve them in a crock with sugar for the winter. Charity told the rest of the women as she had to get to work at the laundry. The rest decided to go spend the day picking blueberries as they didn't know what they were going to use for fruit during the winter. Temperance was used to fruit growing practically year around and so were the three girls from San Francisco. It didn't grow there, but was brought in on ships or by wagon from farther inland or south. Charity was not used to fruit in the winter as she originally was from Kansas.

When her father remarried, she ran away less than a year later and was soon picked up by the man she thought was going to marry her. She had not much luxury of any type in her short life. Living in this house and helping Temperance was the closest to elegance as she had ever been.

The morning was cool but not cold, so the young women only wore light clothing and carried buckets up the hill beyond town. When they found the blueberries, they quickly started picking and quite a bit of eating. As the day progressed, they lost track of time. The oriental girls all wore large brimmed hats to keep the sun off their faces and long gloves to protect their hands and arms. Soon Temperance wished she had done the same. There weren't too many biting bugs but the sun was intense.

Sue Lee had picked farther over toward some trees when the rest heard a small gasp from her. Looking up, they spotted a very large bear standing in the edge of the trees, watching them. Sue Lee was still carrying her bucket, backing slowly toward the rest of the group. Temperance uncoiled her ever present whip.

The bear looked at them and started picking berries. The women slowly backed out of the patch, not a one leaving their bucket behind. There was already many hours of work represented in those buckets.

The bear started toward them once more, not fast, but steadily gaining on their slow backward progress. Temperance popped her whip close to its nose. The bear stopped and backed a step or so, then came forward again. They repeated that two more times and then the bear didn't stop, it just kept walking toward them.

The next pop took a patch of skin off the bears' tender nose. The bear jumped back and rushed back into the trees. The women continued on down the hill and were soon back at the house.

The buckets felt like they were loaded with rocks instead of berries by the time the women set them down.

Temperance was reaching towards her ankles when Pearl asked what she was doing.

"I'm checking to see if I can scratch my ankles without bending over. I think that bucket stretched my arms."

Jasmine, Pearl and Sue Lee collapsed on the floor laughing. Temperance had a huge smile on her face when Luke walked in.

Luke smiled just to see all the women in such good spirits. "You have some really good sunburn going, you might want to put some cool water on your face and arms to stop it from getting worse. Looks like only Jas, Pearl and Sue have enough sense to cover up in the sun."

When they told him about the bear, he warned them that bears could be very dangerous and they really should carry a gun.

"But Luke, I don't have a gun," Temperance told him, "None of us do."

Jasmine went up to the room the women shared and brought down some ointment that she carefully smoothed onto Temperance's face. The burn seemed to ease out as she smoothed it on. Her parents owned a restaurant and used it in the kitchen for burns.

She had found a jar of it in the boxes of supplies from Doc's room. The bundle was full of items from her parents, so she hoped that meant they did not know what her life would have been with the man that bought her. When they searched through the rest of the boxes, each girl had found the bundles she had brought from home. It was nice having at least a few of their own personal belongings.

Temperance found lots of reasons to spend time in the cellar. The cool room soothed any remaining burn on her face and arms. She brought up empty crocks to fill with the berries picked which were then lowered in the cellar to be placed on shelves along the walls. The girls took turns pounding sugar from the cone they were using to add to the berries. When Charity came home for lunch, she taught all the others how to make pie crust and they soon had several pies baking in the oven. While the oven was hot, they added a roaster of meat and some vegetables to have for dinner that night. Roast would be a welcome change.

Sue Lee put a pot of rice on to cook. It had been a while since the girls had any of the staple of their diet at home. She prepared a large pot so it would last for several days.

Charity was working hard every day now at the Laundry, helping Mattie. Temperance and the other young ladies wandered over the hillsides, finding nice bushes she didn't know the names of, then digging them up and bringing them home to transplant in the yard to start the design she wanted for decorating their home. Gary told her what several of them were, when she asked.

They planted a hedge of rose bushes around the outer edge of the future yard. Temperance thought maybe the thorns would make it work as a fence, also. Luke had not noticed what the ladies were doing until he returned home in the middle of the afternoon to find them all sweaty, digging holes in the yard and carrying buckets of water from the creek to water the latest additions to his yard.

When he finally looked around, he whistled. For being delicate looking little ladies, these had done a vast amount of hard manual labor, including his lady wife.

Gary had found a wheelbarrow somewhere for them and they used it all over the hillside, dragging back plants to replant. Then they found the irises along the creek above any working mines and dug up all they could find, along with violets. The area would be ruined later by mining so at least they could keep the flowers alive. Some of the other plants looked like they might be flowers too, so were added to their loads.

The heavy black soil along the upper creek banks was brought back in smaller loads in the wheelbarrow. They added it to the dirt they were digging out to transplant into and liked the looks of it.

Small trees now graced each corner. Luke asked Temperance if she was leaving any on the hills. Then he found her blueberry patch. She told him she didn't like competing with bears.

Sue Lee was doing most of the cooking now with the other two assisting when they were not roaming the hillside digging up plants.

The yard was beginning to look like a wild parkland. Luke had never seen one quite like it, but he thought it looked very nice. Gary built a picnic table under the clump of mature birch still in the yard.

Then the August rains started. All the work on the house was finished and Gary and his crew were all paid in full. Luke asked him if he had any other jobs lined up yet and he said he had promised Mattie he would try to enclose her laundry before winter hit.

Luke was working every day on his mining claims. He was always a dirty mess when he returned home so was sending his work clothes to Mattie. He knew she would have trouble continuing working once the weather turned so he offered his crew to Gary to assist in getting the laundry framed in and roofed.

So far, the rain had only been occasional showers so the men got in and quickly framed out the building. Then they put the roof on over the bare frame. If she didn't have to worry about the tent leaking on her drying clothes, she would be happier. Almost all the men in town used Mattie's services at the laundry, so there were many willing hands to do the building and enclosing her large tent.

Reggie Morse watched from a distance, his mind full of black thoughts as he watched his dream crumble into the mud of the street.

Chapter 8

Reggie had convinced himself he would have soon become a wealthy man just like that fancy pants young snob with all the women. One of the drovers that drove a wagon for him when he returned with his wife had told Reggie that whiskey was from the supply Doc was bringing up.

Doc had to have managed to buy women for their venture. That was the only way they could make a fortune. Where were they? He felt the talks he and Doc used to hold over a bottle made him Doc's heir. Somebody owed him some women and whiskey. No, he didn't have any money invested in the venture, but he and Doc were going to work the saloon together. Doc could have had an accident later, after they were established and no one would have questioned him continuing to run the place.

Then there was Mattie. Why hadn't she just sold him the property? Right after her little "accident" she had been almost talked into selling but then that red headed gal stepped in to help and was getting the chance of a partnership out of it. He should have offered to help her but he cringed at the thought of all that hard work. Why did everyone else have all the luck? He had offered to

80

marry Mattie but she would have nothing to do with him and actually threw a pan of water on him to get him to leave the tent. Once they were married, he could have closed down the laundry and set up the saloon right there in that big old tent. Now it was going to be a big barn of a building. She would have room to dry clothes in the winter and even put in an area for bathes. She had a big old pitcher pump set up in there and huge vats for heating water. Even now she had a crew out cutting firewood for her.

He dreamed of how those vats could be put to better use making beer. How about whisky? Maybe he could even make whiskey. His Pa used to make his own whiskey.

While he stood there and dreamed on, he was scratching at the scabs left from his last time visiting the tent. He also dreamed of revenge. Someday he would have his revenge on those two. Maybe even the redhead. He didn't know how, but he would be working on a plan.

He almost had himself convinced Mattie would have married him if the others had taken longer to get here. He had worked hard to make the trail to the creek where she used to dip water extremely slick between her trips back and forth. He finally added melted lard to the mud to assure it was super slick. He managed to do that without anyone even seeing him.

He figured if she couldn't work, she would turn to him for help and support. He stopped in the next day, only to have her throw the water at him when he was trying to be nice to her. Maybe once she agreed to marry him, he

81

would get one of his friends to pretend to be a preacher and perform the wedding, then leave town. He would play the doting husband until he got the saloon up and running then he would laugh at her and dump her out in the street.

His daydreams entertained him very well and he was leaning against a tree, chortling to himself. Gary OldMan came up behind him and saw the way he was watching the building and Mattie and listened to him mumbling under his breath a while, then clapped him on the back and asked why he wasn't lending a hand?

Reggie almost swallowed his own tongue. Geez, how long had HE been standing behind him?

"What do you think you're doing, sneaking around, listening in on a man's private thoughts?" he grumbled.

"If they are so private, maybe you ought to keep quiet about them. If anything were to happen to that building or that woman that owns it, there would be a lot of very unhappy people around here." Gary told him. "You would probably be the very first suspect."

Reggie paled considerably. He was well aware of what an unhappy group of Miners could do if they were upset. He had participated in a couple of rail parties and a hanging years ago.

"I would never do anything to Mattie, we are in love and she is going to marry me," he told OldMan.

"Is she aware of this?" Gary asked him.

"Of course she is. We just been keeping it quiet so no one gets the wrong idea around here. Seems a lot of folks get their exercise by jumping to conclusions," he said.

"If you say so," then Gary went on down to the Laundry to continue working on it.

When Mattie brought around a large pot of coffee and a mug to see if he wanted some, he considered asking her outright if she was going to marry that no-account Reggie. He was a private man himself and didn't want to embarrass her if what Reggie said was true. He smiled at her and accepted the coffee.

"I seen you talking to that pimple on the backside of the world Reggie, a bit ago. Why is he hanging around here anyway? I thought we sent him packing the other day."

Well now, that certainly didn't sound like a woman in love and about to be married, did it? Gary thought about it as he sipped at the scalding hot coffee.

"He was telling me about you two being in love and going to get married here, soon," Gary told her.

"HE WHAT?"

Gary held his free hand over his ear, the lady had very good lungs. He was afraid she was going to have apoplexy over the thought of marrying Reggie.

"So, I take it he isn't telling the truth or you are upset that he let the cat out of the bag so to speak?"

She rounded on Gary and for a minute, he thought she was going to smack him with the hot coffee pot.

"I would sooner marry a rabid polecat, not that there are any in Alaska, but to put it mildly, no, I am not marrying that little sneaky varmint. He has been a pain in my backside ever since I turned Doc down about selling this place to him for a saloon. Reggie was hanging on Doc's coattails all the time and never had a dime to his own

name and not about to do any honest work to earn one
Ask him to do some simple job for you and see what he
does."

Mattie stomped off with her coffee pot and mug. Just
wait until she saw Reggie again, spreading rumors like that.

She didn't have very long to wait. The next morning as
she was opening the door on her new building, Reggie
sidled up beside her and handed her a handful of wild
flowers he had yanked out of the ground when he saw
them on his way over to waylay her before anyone else
showed up.

She didn't even hesitate, she swung from the hip and
punched Reggie in the chin, lifting him off his feet. Mattie
had worked hard all her life, Reggie had done few honest
jobs and the days of physical labor could be counted on
one hand. He was out for the count.

She dusted her hands together, and left him lying there
with his posey of flowers still clutched in his hand, across
his chest. He looked like he was laid out, as he had
greased back his hair and dressed in his cleanest suit.

A customer came in soon after and asked about him,
she shook her head and said he was a public nuisance,
they should consider hiring a sheriff or something to keep
riffraff off the streets.

Mitch saw him there a few minutes later and came over
to see about moving him away from her door. She
thanked him and went on with her work.

Mitch hauled him over into a shaded area beneath some
trees and left him there. He was breathing and there
wasn't much else to be done for him except maybe throw

some cold water in his face but at least at present, he wasn't bothering anyone.

The next time Mitch looked out his window, Reggie was gone. The man was becoming an irritant.

Mitch watched for Charity and as she walked down the hill from the big house, he walked out to escort her to work. He was becoming attached to this redheaded pretty girl. She never gave any sign of any special feelings for him though and he thought she regarded him as simply a friend. He was patient. He would give her time. He knew she had some kind of story, but he didn't care. She would tell him when she felt like it, if she ever thought of him at all.

Charity did like Mitch, but after her last experience with a man that claimed to love her and asked her to marry him, she was extremely leery of anything more than maybe some sort of friendship. She did not plan on ever getting married. Then she would never have to tell anyone what an idiot she had been.

Charity tried to make sure she did all the heavy lifting and when she walked in and saw Mattie rubbing her knuckles, she was apologetic about not being there earlier. Mattie told her she was still early, Mattie had just encouraged a rat to move on. Her hand was a little sore but it would be fine. Charity looked at her.

"A rat? I didn't even know we had rats here. How did you hurt your hand, did it bite you?"

She grabbed Mattie's hand, checking for teeth marks. All she saw were bruised knuckles. Mattie started laughing.

85

"No, I punched him. The dang rat told Gary we were getting married and I just couldn't help myself. When he showed up here with his hair greased back and some poor wilted looking flowers, I just punched him."

"Which rat would that be?" Charity asked her.

"The worst one, Reggie. That man seems to always be around whenever something bad happens. He was here behind Doc when he asked to buy this place, he was here the day I fell down the bank of the creek. Gary came over after that happened and set up the shallow well and pump so I didn't have to dip all the water used here from the creek and carry it up here. Then he tried burning the tent the day your friend Temperance peeled some hide off him with her whip. Dang, sure wish I knew how to use one like that. I could have marked him up a bit more. He still has scabs and don't leave them alone, always picking at them. The man has said he is going to marry me. I can just imagine how that would go. Me working to support his scrawny little butt or him arranging an accident so he could have his saloon here."

Mattie finally wound down and sat on the bench they had placed against one side of the door. Charity sat down beside her and placed a basin of water beside her to soak her sore hand in.

"Do you think you would ever consider getting married? I thought I was going to be married once." Charity told her.

Mitch was about to walk in but halted in mid stride. Whoa, this was what he was interested in. Charity stayed quiet and then Mattie told her she had been married once, many years ago but her husband was killed in a fight over in Dawson. Charity then told Mattie about her fiancé selling her to Doc. Mattie looked at her in amazement. "Can we go find your fiancé and cut him into little bitty pieces and feed him to something?"

At the door, Mitch was feeling the same way. He would make her forget that loser and then he stepped back. How could he let her know he didn't care about her past, he only cared that her future included him.

He tapped lightly on the door, then stepped in. "How are you lovely ladies doing this morning? I notice the yard ornament has left, Mattie. You sure you don't want me to arrange a little party for him? I'm sure plenty of the men would be more than happy to help him move on to another town."

Charity gave him a hard look. Had he been at the door when she told Mattie her secret? He smiled at her and she relaxed. No decent man would still look at her after hearing about her past. Mitch was as decent as they got.

Mitch dropped off his laundry and left soon after. Mattie looked at Charity, "That man likes you a lot. You could do a lot worse than to encourage him to like you even more."

"Mattie, he is too decent for the likes of me."

"Nonsense. Nothing that has happened to you was your fault. Even if you made some decisions that led to bad things, you were little more than a kid at the time and your pa certainly didn't stick up for you with your stepma. If you can't believe a man that says he loves you and wants to marry you, who can you trust?"

"I didn't know him very well. I fell for a handsome face and smooth talking. I think if I ever decide to marry, I want to be very good friends first and know the man extremely well for quite a while."

"That's how it was for me and my man. We grew up in the same little town and knew each other from childhood on. He was always my best friend, we could talk about anything. Looks change and can go away, character and friendship doesn't. Don't settle for less."

Charity started the first batch of clothes going through the vats steaming on the fires. The blacksmith was building hoods to go over each vat to carry the smoke out of the building. He would be installing them in a few days. Until then the smoke stayed in the rafters and they worked through.

Chapter 9

Now there were some different berries ripe on the hills around Paradise. These were small, red, very tart berries that jelled very well. Luke called them cranberries. Temperance and the other young women planned an outing to pick berries for the weekend. Luke gave Temperance a rifle to take along with them for protection. Then he decided to go along and help carry buckets back as well as pick.

It was a slow day at the laundry, so Mattie and Charity came along also. Mitch wasn't open on weekends so they ended up making a party of it. Gary OldMan joined them as they started hiking up the hill. He carried a far heavier rifle than the one Luke had given Temperance. When Luke asked him about it, he said "Grizzly" in a very low voice. "No use scaring the ladies, but there has been one seen on the hills back here recently."

Luke and Mitch each carried baskets of food for a lunch later. The women each carried a bucket. Mitch thought they were being over-zealous estimating the berry picking until he saw the carpet of berries in the moss under the birch trees.

The baskets were placed under some trees and everyone started picking in earnest. These berries were much firmer than the blueberries so Temperance had a couple of bags that she dumped buckets into as they picked. When they stopped for lunch the bags were as full as she planned on filling them. She tied the tops shut then tied the bags together so they could be placed over a shoulder and leave hands free.

The group chatted and laughed all the time they were picking and Gary figured they would not have a problem with any bear coming around.

After everyone was done eating, they resumed picking and in a couple of hours the buckets were full enough also.

Gary carried his and Mattie's buckets down the hill. Luke put the two tied bags over his shoulder along with his empty backpack that lunch had traveled in and carried his and Temperance's buckets. Mitch carried his and Charity's buckets which left Jasmine, Pearl and Sue Lee struggling along with theirs. Mattie, Temperance and Charity each helped one of the women and although it was awkward to walk with two people holding one bucket handle, they managed to get down the hill without mishap.

The women were laughing and talking up ahead of the men when a shot rang out. Everyone dropped to the ground. No one knew if it was someone out hunting that didn't know they were in the area or if it was fired with intent to hurt someone. Gary spoke in a low voice, "Is everyone okay?"

Muted assurances answered him.

No one moved and soon they heard movement on the hill above and to the right of their present location. Soon Gary spotted Josh Wilcox moving toward them through the brush and small trees. He raised his rifle and fired a shot into the tree right beside Josh's head.

"Hey, what do you think you are doing? There is a bear down, here between you and me. Help me find it."

Gary left his buckets and slowly made his way toward Josh, keeping his rifle loosely held pointing toward Josh. One wrong move and he would be history.

They searched the area and didn't find a bear. However there were tracks so Gary decided to give Josh the benefit of the doubt on the shot toward them, this time.

"Hey, I'm sorry I didn't see you before I shot. All I was thinking was a nice warm fur blanket for winter and fresh meat in camp," Josh said.

"Just be careful, alright? We don't need any accidents," Gary told him.

Josh was still searching around for sign of where his bear went as Gary walked back down to the group below.

"I may be sorry later, but somehow I believe him on this one," Gary told them. "There were tracks and then the bear suddenly jumped and ran, like it was spooked. Could have been the shot. Josh is usually not good at telling tales, so I think this time it was the truth."

"Was there any sign that the bear was injured?" Luke asked.

"No, no sign of blood at all. I think it was a clean miss."

The group resumed their trek to the house and soon had the berries in the kitchen. Gary showed them a quick

92

way to clean the berries, by placing a wide board sloping down into a large tub, covering it with a towel, then pouring the berries down the towel. The berries rolled into the tub, the twigs, moss and leaves stayed on the towel.

As soon as Mattie's bucket was cleaned, Gary offered to help her carry it home. He said he needed to get a few things done at home also and would clean his berries at home. After they left, the women cleaned the rest of the berries and stored them dry in open crocks in the cellar. They would keep all winter.

Later in the day, they heard more shots from the hills behind town. Since almost everyone in town hunted for grouse, ptarmigan or hares, besides moose and bears, no one ever paid any attention to the sound of shooting.

When Charity showed up at work the next morning, Mattie thanked her for including her in their outing. She had fun, got a winter's supply of berries and even enjoyed Gary's company. She figured that was because he was straight forward and never even acted like more than a friend. She thought he was sweet on one of the other girls but he never let on.

The crew Luke hired to fill their woodshed with wood for the winter were doing a fine job. They cut trees, then used the horses to drag them to the yard and cut them to length, then stacked in the shed. Wood piles were sprouting all around town, too.

Near the end of August, it started getting dark for a little while each night. Temperance still wasn't used to going to sleep in daylight, waking during the night and it was still daylight, getting up with the sun already moving around the sky. She welcomed the return of darkness. Luke told her she would soon get more darkness than she had ever seen.

The Northern Lights first scared her, then delighted her. She woke up everyone in the house to see them. Later, Gary told her it was the trail of ancestors hunting in the sky. He also told her not to whistle at them as they might come down and carry her away.

Temperance looked at Luke and he nodded yes, he had heard that, too. Sometimes on high hills, the Lights made noise and raised the hairs on your arms and back of your neck. He wasn't going to whistle and take any chances.

The nights were getting colder and soon there was frost showing in the early morning sunlight. The trees turned gold and here and there brilliant crimson foliage popped out to please the eye. The accents here and there of a deep green spruce added to the patch quilt appearance of the hills.

One morning before the colors were all gone from the trees, they awoke to find the ground covered in snow. Temperance, Pearl, Jasmine and Sue Lee rushed outside to touch it and play in it like children. They had never actually touched snow and had not totally believed what they were told when they first saw snow covered mountains from the ship or even along the trail heading to Paradise. But here it was, right in the front yard and soon they were soaking wet and cold, but still laughing and tossing handfuls of it at each other.

They stood shivering around the stove until Charity
came in the room on her way to work. "Why don't you
all go change into dry clothes? You will all catch your
death of colds standing there waiting for your clothes to
dry and to get warm."

The young women grinned sheepishly at each other and
headed up the stairs. Soon there were soggy clothes
hanging all over near the heater, drying out.

Charity found some of the leftover brick used for
making the chimneys in the house and brought them
indoors to dry thoroughly. Then she started keeping
them on the back of the heater top. When she was ready
to retire for the night, she wrapped one in a towel and
carried it up to warm her bed. Soon the rest of the
women were doing the same thing. She told them her
family always kept some rocks in the edge of the fireplace
to use for bed warmers.

The working mines were closing down for the winter,
so now there were more men out hunting in the woods as
the weather was cool enough for meat to keep. There
were also more men out cutting and hauling firewood
back to town. The first snow had melted away, but from
the look of the sky, that was a temporary condition.
Mitch and Luke were on their way home from hunting
when they heard someone yell a distance off to their left.

They soon found the man that had yelled, standing
there, looking down at the remains of someone half
buried under some debris.

Mitch immediately started looking around for the bear
that had buried its cache of food for later. The jacket

looked like the one Josh usually wore when he was going hunting although no one had seen him around town for a couple of weeks. A rifle lay across the dirt under the body and looked like it had been fired but was now gathering some rust. The body had obviously been there a while.

Luke offered to go get some help and a litter of some kind to place the body on to take it back to town. Mitch said he would stay and keep an eye out for the bear and the other fellow would stay, also.

Luke soon found enough help and they managed to make a litter and headed back up the hill. As they lifted the body, a slug fell onto the ground and the men looked at it in shock. It was a different caliber than the rifle carried by the man they were picking up. Time and scavengers had done too much damage to be able to tell exactly what had killed the man, but the presence of that slug made it pretty positive it had not been either natural causes or a bear.

After they reached town, they had no idea of where to take the body. They didn't have much of a real doctor and there were no funeral parlors or even a church yet in the new town. So far, they had managed to police themselves so there wasn't even a policeman, sheriff or jail.

There were locations on the plat he had made to file on the ground for a town, but so far, no need to actually construct anything. Even the area set aside for a cemetery was uncleared. Now there was need and they would have to get a hole dug very soon or the ground would be frozen too hard and deep until spring. Luke immediately asked if anyone would be willing to dig the grave and maybe dig a couple more before the ground froze. At least the area was marked out and locations marked with stakes on site.

Mattie finally let them place the litter on the floor near her back door to keep the contents as cold as possible. She really didn't want that odor and any leakage to contend with all winter while working in there.

Mitch and Dave started building a casket near the body after Mattie told them "Sure, why not."

As they lifted the body from the litter to place it in the casket, Mitch felt the crackle of paper in a fold of the jacket.

"Hey, Mattie, could you come here a minute please? Seems there is something in his clothes and maybe we need to check them all. Would you mind doing that while we hold it up?"

Mattie pulled out an old envelope and several folded sheets of paper. They were all a bit damp, so she placed them on a shelf near the stove to dry. It appeared the papers had been scooped up from under the body when it was placed on the litter, not actually in the pockets.

As they lowered the body into the casket, another slug fell into the casket. This one was a pistol slug and suggested someone had stood over the injured man and shot him directly in the head. They gently turned the body to see and could see where the back of the skull was shattered. Someone had not shot him by accident, then ran, they had walked over and finished the job.

No matter how they twisted the few facts they knew, this man was the victim of murder. Then Mattie asked them if they were going by the coat and pants and just assuming this was a man?

Mitch looked at Dave. They both turned to look at Mattie. "Aw, no, don't tell us we have to take his clothes off. I can barely stand the smell as it is as he warms up a bit in here." Dave looked green around the edges.

Mattie took pity on Dave and agreed to help Mitch find out if it were truly a man they were about to bury. She unfastened the belt and they carefully pulled the pants down. The evidence was inconclusive. Too much damage by small scavengers to tell for sure. They removed the boots and the feet looked very neat and trim. Not exactly what would be expected of a working man. They were narrow and well cared for. The nails were even quite neatly trimmed although they looked in need of another trim.

Mattie looked at Mitch. "I think we need to remove all the clothing and I think we need other people in here to help and be witnesses."

"I think you are right. If we just say what we think we've found, no one will believe us."

Chapter 10

Dave went to find Gary. Instead, Luke was walking by so both men came back in. When they saw the delicate feet, they both stopped in shock.

"I can say for certain, that is not Josh Wilcox," Luke told them. "We were wading in the pond, trying to clear a log from the overflow pipe and his feet never looked like that."

As they carefully removed the shreds of clothing from the remains in the casket, it became obvious that the clothing had not been on the body when it was killed. There were no bullet holes in the clothing. The body had several. As they progressed, it became obvious this was a woman. Mattie told the men she would take over and they were glad to leave her to it.

When they returned later, the body was now clothed in a plain simple gown and a scarf covered the face and head. Mattie told them the poor woman shouldn't go in her killers' clothes.

As they talked, everyone wondered why someone not only killed a woman, but took the time to redress her? Maybe they thought by the time the body was found, if it ever was, that pieces of clothing would be all that was left to identify it? Who would want to be thought dead?

The only things they were sure of was that someone unknown was dead and not by natural causes. Conjecture added that probably the person responsible was trying to escape punishment by making it look like a bear attack. Then he could disappear to profit from some other crime he had committed or even just this one.

The men decided to return to the scene of the murder and try to find more clues tomorrow. No one thought the murderer would try wearing the victims clothing so maybe it was hidden somewhere close by.

By now the papers found in the folds of the coat were dry enough to carefully spread out and read. One sheet was a map. No one could read the other two pages. Luke said it looked like Spanish. The papers from his wedding agreement fresh in his mind.

"Maybe Temperance can read them. I will ask her when I get home and see if she can read and then if she will come down here and see if it is in Spanish." He felt foolish for not knowing if his wife could even read. He had told her everything about himself and never even asked a simple thing like that about her. Maybe Mattie was right, men were selfish.

When they looked outside the next morning, there was a thin coating of snow over everything. Luke wasn't sure if they would be able to find anything at all, but they would still go try. As he, Dave and Mitch walked up the hill, they watched the woods all around them. For some reason, they all felt like they were being observed. The woods were silent and that was not the usual way of the forest. Birds twittered, argued and scolded and squirrels were always willing to give away the presence of an intruder if a man were walking through, intent on finding something for his table. Today's stillness grated.

The area where the body was found appeared more disturbed than when they were there retrieving the body. Moss was torn and tossed aside, brush was broken over and where the body had lain, the dirt was even dug around in.

The hairs on the back of Luke's neck were giving him reason to think they were in immediate danger and he knew he must look like his head was on a swivel. Dave was on his knees, checking every leaf and twig that had been disturbed.

"I think it was the bear, looking for his cache," he told them.

Then Luke looked closer to the ground as his eyes searched around the area and he saw something else the bear had dug out. Under the moss a few feet away from the area the body had been, a piece of bright cloth was showing against the white of the snow. It would have blended into the fall colors except for the snow.

The men carefully loosened the soil around the cloth and soon uncovered a dress and undergarments. A delicate pair of boots was uncovered last. A small case beside the boots was the last item they found in the shallow hole. If not for the bear and the snow, they would never have found the cache.

They placed everything in the bag they had brought and headed down the hill. Mitch thought he saw movement back in the woods, but wasn't sure and when he tried to point it out to the others, no one else saw anything. It might have been the bear, but it appeared too tall and the wrong shape.

Back at the Laundry, they placed the clothing across the casket to dry out. The dress showed the entry bullet holes very well. There was only one exit wound. The weapon used must have been an older black powder weapon without as much power as modern weapons. Some people still used them. None of the bullets had been the fatal shot until the close range shot by pistol to the head. This was definitely murder.

Temperance came back to the Laundry with Charity after lunch. She was actually very well educated and would see about reading the letters found with the map.

She and Charity looked the dress over and said it was very old fashioned, not something someone from a city or newcomer would be apt to wear. The boots were old but very well made. They looked vaguely European and expensive at one time.

The letters were not in Spanish. Temperance was fairly positive they were in Russian but she was not fluent in Russian and only knew a bit of the writing. The Cyrillic alphabet wasn't one of her strong points and her tutor finally gave up. She could make herself understood for basic needs and that was about it.

"Luke, even though Spaniards may have named some of the landmarks in Alaska along the coast, it was the

103

Russians that claimed it. I am sure you will find many here that understand Russian. I'm not sure whether or not any will be able to read it. It's my understanding they were not much on schooling the peasants or serfs and that is about all they considered the people here."

Dave nodded in agreement.

They opened the bag found with the clothes and carefully went through it. A couple of letters and a bible with the name written in the flyleaf gave the name, Ilena Wiloic. The letters were General Delivery, Holy Cross, Alaska Territory.

Dave told them that was a settlement near the Bering Sea on the Yukon River.

"Because of the coat, I thought it was Josh Wilcox, when we first found it," Luke said.

Temperance told him they might have been related and Wilcox was maybe the Americanized version of Wiloic. Many people did that when they came to America, changing the spelling of their names for various reasons. Maybe this was Josh's sister or wife.

Chapter 11

The man standing back in the trees cursed his luck. First he had dropped the map but didn't notice until later when he was many miles away so he came back, just in time to see the recovery of the remains.

Then the bear had showed up and he didn't dare just shoot it and draw even more attention to this location. The bear had wandered off, then returned several times, each time scaring him off. Then, when the bear finally departed for better pickings and he was almost back to the site, he heard people coming back up the hill.

Damned if they didn't head right for the location he was trying to search. He stood in frustrated silence as they searched and found the clothing he had stashed farther from the body but the bear had uncovered them searching for something to eat by the smell he associated with his earlier meals.

He was still standing there cursing his luck when a twig snapped behind him. He slowly turned around and saw the bear standing only a few feet behind him. He stood up as tall as he could and held his coat out to the sides trying to make himself appear much bigger than he actually was. The bear looked him over and stomped his front feet at him, then slowly turned and started away.

The bear walked a few feet, then whirled and stomped his feet at the man yet again. Sweat was popping out on the man's forehead as the bear was deciding just what to do.

As the bear again slowly turned away, the man stepped carefully backward away from the bear, trying to increase the distance. This bear had tasted human flesh and did not seem to mind possibly having seconds.

Each time the bear mock charged, the man stood his ground and sweated. Each time the bear turned his back, the man stepped back and after a while, the bear tired of playing and just continued walking away. It had been a good berry year and the bear was not actually hungry, a snack before hibernating would be fine but unnecessary.

The man decided he was pressing his luck enough just coming back to look for the map and papers, he would see if he could redraw the map from memory and maybe he could still find what it told of. He doubted if anyone here could read Polish, anyway.

He hesitated when he reached the top of the hill and contemplated going into town or continuing on the trail that would take him to Tanana. From Tanana, he could catch a boat on down river and resupply for his search. Maybe even find a couple of men to use as packers. They could always be disposed of, later. This was a large unsettled wilderness, he should be able to find better areas to dispose of unwanted encumbrances.

He did not notice the man sitting back off the trail, waiting for a moose. He had a plan now and was intent on putting it in motion before the heavy snows started that would lock him into staying in place for most of the winter. He was patient, up to a point. Waiting for Ilena had wasted almost the entire summer. He did not intend on waiting too much longer.

The man waiting for a moose saw the other man walk by. "Hmmmm, wonder what he's doing back in the country? Haven't seen him around for quite a while and he looks to be in a hurry to be somewhere else right now. Well, maybe he will have better luck somewhere else."

He tired of waiting and started walking back toward town. With no particular rush to be back in town, he meandered along, finally finding that he was on the man's back trail so followed him back to how he had spent the morning. He found the dance with the bear and was surprised to see that he was near the place the body was found. He studied the tracks a while and pondered on any significance it might have to the murder. He would talk it over with Luke some time when he had a chance.

Chapter 12

The funeral was very short as no one knew the departed and there were no Preachers in town. There wasn't even a church yet. Only the people that had found the body attended, with Mattie and Charity coming to show support. As town founder, Luke read a Bible verse and said a few words about the unexpected death. Then the casket was lowered and the men filled the dirt back in the hole.

When Mattie and Charity returned to the laundry to work, Charity started sniffling. Mattie awkwardly patted her on the back and went on with the washing.

"It's just so sad to think a woman was murdered up there and no one was even here to mourn for her or family to grieve about her untimely passing. That could happen to any of us being up here away from family and friends we grew up with. If Temperance had not befriended me on that ship, I could have met the same fate." Charity was still sniffling so Mattie barely heard her.

"Yes, that could happen to any one of us. Most people up here have come from somewhere else and no one is immune to sudden death. I hate to think whoever did that is getting away with it scott free." Mattie told her.

They worked in silence, each deep in her own thoughts, interrupted once in a while by a customer coming in. Laundry was always being picked up or dropped off.

Mitch came in to see if Charity was ready to go home. Both women were surprised to see it was past quitting time for the day. When they stepped outside, they were unprepared for the snow blowing in their faces. There was already a few inches on the ground and the wind was blowing it into drifts that could become quite a problem by morning. The heavy clouds made it almost dark and as they hurried up the hill toward the big house, Mitch had to grab Charity's arm several times to keep the wind from knocking her over.

By the time they reached the front door, Charity was puffing from the unexpected exertion. It had taken a lot of strength to fight the snow and the wind just to make it home.

The snow covering them was thick enough that until Mitch spoke, Jasmine wasn't sure just who had entered the house right in front of her. For one brief moment, she thought they were ghosts. Then she rushed over to help Charity remove her hat, coat and gloves. Then she turned to Mitch and took his hat and coat to hang near the heater to dry out. This was an early snow and the temperatures were still warm enough for it to be a heavy wet snow. She shooed Charity upstairs to change so she wouldn't chill and told her to be sure to bring her shoes back down to dry by the stove.

Charity was only too happy to comply. She felt chilled to the bone and was unsure whether or not she would have managed the trip home without Mitch's help. After working in the laundry all day, she was always tired by evening. Tonight, she felt like she had been wrung out like the heavy clothes were, to dry.

Dinner was on the table by the time she came back downstairs. The hot stew and biscuits was perfect for the cold evening. Everyone ate with gusto and most took seconds.

Temperance still was not quite used to the table manners of these Americans. They ate their meals at odd times of the day and didn't seem to mind the lack of servants or a meal served in courses.

Her Grandfather would have termed them all savages and uncivilized. Maybe they were, but she liked having everyone sharing the table and all talking about their day. People reaching or asking to have a dish passed was something she had never seen before. Grandfather would have had a heart attack if one of the hired help had sat down to table with him. He thought nothing of keeping one waiting, hat in hand while he leisurely ate his meal and had a cigar after. He was Lord and Master of his universe and no one was allowed to forget it.

She rather liked the relaxed atmosphere of their table. Everyone laughed, talked and enjoyed their meal. The day was not broken up by a siesta, either and she found she preferred this way of doing things. The days were growing shorter and now she could say she worked from before sunup until after sundown. It sounded so much like she was overworked, she laughed as she wrote it in her journal.

112

Temperance awoke with a start. Something downstairs had made a crashing sound. She reached for Luke but found only the empty side of the bed. The crash came again and she hurriedly dressed and grabbed her ever present whip. It was such an automatic response she never realized she did it. She grabbed the small pistol Luke had given her in the other hand.

Wearing only heavy socks on her feet, she eased toward the stairs. As she edged slowly down them, she could see a glow from the formal parlor. No one ever used that room as it was cold and the furniture was not all that comfortable. She searched each room as she made her way to the parlor, trying to find if anything was out of place. It was not all that uncommon in California to have bandits break into nice homes and rob or kidnap people. She wasn't sure if that happened here, but thought there was always a first time. She would rather be safe than sorry.

As she neared the parlor, she heard low voices. Someone was very angry and she felt a chill down her back. The voice was one she had heard in California, late one night, talking to her Grandfather. Diego! What was he doing here? The man truly scared her. She was positive her Grandfather had been paying him off to leave them alone, but the man always looked at her like he was gauging her age, size and weight like he was bidding on her.

Now he was in her parlor and from the sounds, he was beating on someone. She inched forward and saw Diego draw back to hit Luke yet again. She could not believe her

113

eyes, Luke was bound to a chair and unable to help himself. As Diego started to swing, Temperance didn't even stop to think, she shot him. A movement to her right brought the whip into play and popped the man starting toward her. Then shot the man behind Luke that was drawing a knife. Diego sat moaning on the floor, holding a small but painful flesh wound, as she rushed over to Luke's side. She grabbed up the knife the man behind him had dropped and slashed the ropes binding him to the chair.

She felt Diego's hand close around her ankle as Luke slid forward in the chair. It was too close to use the whip so she tried pulling lose from him. By this time the other women in the house were running down the stairs and into the parlor.

Charity had the stove poker in her hand and laid out the man Temperance had hit with the whip. Then she saw Diego and cracked him a good one with the poker, also. His hand loosened around her ankle and she sat down on the floor beside Luke.

Her ankle was throbbing but Luke looked like he had been run over by a team of horses. The man Temperance had shot was edging toward the door when Pearl slid her little sharp knife toward his throat, he stopped and held very still. Jasmine and Sue Lee started tying hands and feet. Pearl and Charity came over to see what they could do to help Temperance and Luke. Pearl stepped out the door and scooped up a bowl of snow. They used it on Luke's face to take down the swelling and on Temperance's ankle the same way.

114

They asked the least injured of the men how they had got there and he remained quiet, then Jasmine stepped over and whispered in his ear and he started telling them everything they wanted to know.

They had the old man out in a wagon and it had been a hard trip making it here from the coast. There were no good roads and the trails were filling in with snow.

"What old man?" Temperance asked.

"Your Grandfather. You were supposed to be Diego's. He has been waiting many years for you to grow up. Then that old fool let this Gringo have you," the man snarled.

"My Grandfather is outside in this weather? Where is the wagon?"

"With any luck, he has frozen by now. He is a most disagreeable man. The wagon is parked just down the hill a ways, near a large building that blocked some of the wind," the man told her.

Charity and the other three quickly dressed as warmly as possible and started down the hill to see about rescuing her Grandfather. Luke still was unconscious and the others were all patched up and tied securely. Temperance sat beside Luke and kept a pack of snow in a cloth over the worst of his bruises. His eyes flickered open and he looked up into her face.

"I must be dead, I'm seeing an Angel," he told her.

Charity came back in, followed by the other three women.

"We got Mitch and Gary to take care of your Grandfather and the horses. They took him into the

Laundry and Mattie is overseeing thawing him out in one of her vats. He is okay, just mad and unpleasant. I didn't think you needed to put up with that tonight and Mattie said she would put his head underwater if he didn't correct his language so he has. Mitch and Gary said they will spend the night in the Laundry with him. Mattie told them to keep the fire stoked then, she was going to bed," Charity told them.

"What are we going to do with these three?"

"Three? Where is the fourth man? There were four when they came in," Luke said.

Luke and Temperance stayed where they were, he wrapping her ankle and she cleaning up his face, while the other four women searched the entire house. No one wanted to go down into the cellar so they rolled one of the heavy barrels over the trap door and decided that could be done in the daylight. Then they helped Luke and Temperance up the stairs to their room. This time, the doors were all bolted firmly shut. They had gotten out of the habit.

Mitch and Gary were helping Temperance's Grandfather in the door as she hobbled down the stairs the next morning. He immediately said something to her that caused her face to blanch and Gary smacked the old man firmly on the shoulder.

"You be nice to her. She is hurt, her husband is hurt, all because of you. We can always take you back down to let Mattie oversee your return to the coast. After the way you treated her, I am sure it would be a most pleasant trip."

116

It was Fernando's turn to become pale. He shut up and they helped him on into the kitchen where both stoves were going and Sue Lee was preparing breakfast. He started ordering her around and she stepped up to him with her knife in hand.

"You are here because you are Temperance's Grandfather. We would have treated you with respect because of her, but if you don't learn that we are all free people, helping out here, then you will no longer be treated well. I understand you are the reason she is hurt. That means from now on, you have to earn your respect."

Fernando looked like he was going to explode, but held his tongue. Twice being told to behave was a new experience for him. He was always the one everyone kowtowed to. To be told by a woman was unthinkable, however the look in her eyes and the way she held the knife gave him pause. Then she set the knife down and he stepped closer.

"I demand an apology."

"Demand away, you may get one when you earn one," and she turned her back on him to continue preparing the meal.

He grabbed her shoulder and started to pull her around and she threw him. She had not been the workout dummy for all her brothers without learning how to protect herself.

He landed hard on the floor and she stood there looking at him as if daring him to try anything else. He thought it over and decided he would bide his time.

Everyone was polite to him but no one started a conversation with him and no one stayed to listen to him. He was unpleasantly surprised to see that everyone sat at the table to eat and food was passed around the table. Evidently, there were no servants.

While eating breakfast, they could hear a muffled banging. Soon someone remembered the fourth man from last night and they finished breakfast before checking to see if he indeed was in the cellar.

When they finally rolled the barrel off the cellar door, the man shut in below was so cold he could barely make it up the steps. He looked like he wanted to hug the stoves. The cellar was barely above freezing and his coat had been discarded near the front door when they came in last night.

Once he was able to talk again, he stammered out a story about joining up with the others on their way here from Valdez. They claimed they were going to collect on an old debt. He thought the debt had something to do with the old man's son.

Luke made it downstairs in time to hear the conversation and turned to the old man still seated at the kitchen table.

"Welcome to my home. Is what this man says, true?"

The old man sat as still as a statue but after a few minutes of silence while everyone looked at him, he squirmed a bit and said, "Yes, it is true. My son was not all that I hoped he would be. He made many bad choices and a wager made with Diego was one of the worst.

How does a man live with himself after using his only daughter as the stakes in a wager with a man like that?"

The stranger spoke up, "well, if it makes you feel any better, Diego laughed about rigging the outcome so he should have lost the wager but won it, instead. He was afraid your son would find out and arranged his death. He thought it was all a great joke."

The old man slumped in his chair. What his son had done was still unconscionable but at least he thought it was a sure thing. Rage at his son and Diego sprang to life in the old man.

"Where is Diego? I would like to speak to him," he said.

"At present, we are keeping them in the unfinished town outhouse. We stuck a stove in there and some wood for them. If they manage to climb up out of the hole, they can probably escape, but where will they go and how will they survive? We did not leave any coats with them, they each have one blanket."

Jasmine and Pearl were giggling over by the stove where they were finishing up the dishes.

Chapter 13

Luke wanted to be there when they interrogated the prisoners and said his head was feeling good enough to walk down the hill just to see how they had arranged the jail in the outhouse.

Maybe this should remain a jail and they could start over in a new location for a public outhouse.

When they reached the door, it was ajar. Someone had come in ahead of them. They proceeded with caution and soon heard the sound of voices from inside.

Mitch took one side of the partition and Luke took the other, with guns drawn.

They were surprised to see Mattie, sitting on a stool she must have brought, talking to the men huddled around the stove down in the hole. The hole was about ten by sixteen feet and over six feet deep, so they had plenty of room.

"Mattie, what are you doing here?"

"I heard the sound of digging as I walked by so I came in and settled the boys right down. Me and old Bessie here know how to keep order."

Mitch noticed the old double barrel shotgun loosely aimed in the direction of the prisoners across her lap.

"I would think they would have respect for old Bessie, anyway. I've seen you shoot with that and I wouldn't want to be on the wrong end."

"I think that Diego might need a few pellets dug out of his sorry hide. He didn't think a mere woman would dare shoot him. He was halfway up over the side of that there hole when I walked in. He's lucky I aimed beside him or you would be able to see daylight through him by now. I probably should have, just on general principles."

As she moved toward the door, she had one more suggestion, "Why not make them go cut wood for their stove? Why should someone else have to cut the wood to keep them warm? They don't mind burning it like it is unlimited around here."

As they tried to figure out what to do with the prisoners, Mattie's suggestion kept popping up. Why not let them pay for their own keep? It's not like there were any actual lawmen around or Courts either, for that matter. It might deter crooks from even coming to their town if it got a reputation as hard on criminals. They really wanted to let people know crime did not pay.

Since Luke was still not looking too good from the beating he received the night before, Gary and Mitch would escort the prisoners out on a wood cutting detail. Their horses and wagon would be used to haul the wood back to keep them warm at night. Luke would try seeing about making the place harder to escape from.

After they left to cut wood, Luke visited the blacksmith shop. He suggested leg irons with a heavy ball attached. It would make it much harder to climb out if they had all that extra weight dragging besides the short chain between the ankle bracelets.

By the time the weary prisoners returned that evening, their quarters had been renovated a bit. They now had cots and the promised leg irons. They could shuffle short steps with difficulty. They might be able to climb out, but how would they manage to escape and the iron around their ankles would possibly freeze to the flesh. At present, staying in the warm hole was their best bet for survival.

The supplies on their wagon had enough food to prepare meals for them for a while. Mattie said she didn't mind as she kept the fire going in the Laundry all the time and a pot of beans set on the stove wouldn't take up too much room. She didn't know how to make tortillas so made cornbread for them from the meal.

After several days of this, one of the men asked if he could make the tortillas. Mitch escorted him to the Laundry and Sue Lee and Charity kept an eye on him and learned how to make tortillas also while they were doing it. Mattie thought that was a fine way to use the corn flour and soon the man was showing them all how to do it.

Jose was a large simple man and easily led. Diego kept him around for muscle and because he followed orders no matter what, not knowing any better. He also happened to be a good cook. He always had a smile and seemed about the mental age of a child.

Once away from Diego, he was pleasant to be around. Mattie started borrowing him to help with the heavy work in the Laundry. He enjoyed the work.

Temperance's ankle was back to normal size and the bruising was fading away. Her Grandfather in the house added tension. She was used to having to obey him and was finding it hard to break the habit. Finally Luke told her she did not have to jump to the old man's orders. He was capable of waiting on himself and she was now Luke's wife and as such, answered only to Luke, not her Grandfather.

Finally during dinner one night when the old man snapped an order at Temperance, Luke smacked his fist down on the table making everyone jump.

"That's enough, Fernando. Temperance is my wife now and does not need to listen to any more of your claptrap. If you cannot be pleasant in my home, you may go join your 'friend' Diego. I am used to the pleasant happy surroundings of my friends and wife during dinner and I do not appreciate you ordering people around. Especially not my wife. Which will it be, a warm comfortable room, good food, nice people around you or the hole down the hill with the group you brought down on us, living in an outhouse hole for the rest of the winter?"

"You wouldn't dare treat ME in such a manner."

"Oh? And why wouldn't I? You have not been a nice house guest. You complain about everything. You still order people around. You eat our food, use our wood to heat yourself, expect your laundry to suddenly appear, clean and in your wardrobe. Just why are we supposed to supply you with all the comforts in exchange for you being a thoroughly disagreeable guest? Everyone here in this household contributes something to the good of the household. You are the only freeloader. Make up your mind. Are you going to straighten up or are you joining Diego?"

The old man was livid. No one had ever spoken to him like that. He was an important man. His family was one of the finest in Seville. These Americans. None of that meant anything to them. He should have dismissed the Gringo when he asked to marry Temperance and just kept her for Diego no matter that he did not approve of Diego, either. The thought of all that money and a share in a gold mine had blinded him to the consequences of his actions.

Niggling in the back of his mind was the knowledge of letting Diego have her would have meant her death, one way or another.

Temperance was shocked. She had never had someone take her side in anything. It didn't matter that Luke referred to her as his property. That was a given in this day and age. However, he never treated her like that. He seemed to actually value her opinion and he certainly had thanked her for saving him. He treated her more as an equal which was not something she had ever expected.

She had fallen back into the old habit of obeying her Grandfather. Now she would try not to immediately jump to follow his orders. It would sure make her days easier not to be waiting on the old man. He was in perfect health and capable of doing things for himself but thought nothing of calling her away from making bread or pies to ask her to fetch him a different book from the

125

library which he was sitting closer to than she was, from the kitchen. When she thought about it, she got angry and figured maybe, knowing Luke sided with her, that she could tell him to get it himself.

More than once, her batch of sourdough had to be started over as she would be away from it too long, trying to find just the book her Grandfather wanted. First she had to clean her hands, then search and carry, wait for him to check and see if it were the right book, then return it and get him another. He could take hours picking out a book. If she brought more than one book, he got irate.

Charity had already told him she didn't see no anchor tied to his butt, to get what he wanted himself. He was shocked but never told her to get anything for him again.

If he had ever asked instead of ordered, he would have been treated politely and his request probably filled. Being ordered about brought out the worst in everyone.

Jasmine, Pearl and Sue Lee avoided him whenever possible. He still considered them servants or slaves, they weren't sure which as he was very unpleasant to them all. They were hoping Luke put him down with Diego.

`The next day Fernando kept to himself and the household ran much more smoothly. The women were able to finish the baking and cleaning without fetching and carrying for him.

He sat in the library, fuming. He was someone to be respected and feared. The people here neither respected nor feared him. Then he thought about all that had been said. His actions did not instill respect.

His grandsons were safely shipped off to a school in Seville and his granddaughter was married to a wealthy man that evidently overlooked her bad manners and propensity for getting into trouble, so for the first time in a very long time, he was free of responsibility. If he wanted, he could travel, thanks to that same husband of his granddaughter.

Everyone noticed his improved attitude. Most were afraid to say something in case he changed back into the irritable and irritating person he had been since arriving. Charity wanted to ask him if he had finally planned how to get rid of them all and was contemplating their demise. She didn't think anything else would improve his outlook on life.

When he complimented her on something she prepared, she asked him if he was ill. He didn't know what to reply.

The prisoners down at the outhouse were not enjoying their time. They were cutting wood every day. Winter was closing in hard and the snow depths were making it difficult for the horses to pull the wagon around to pick up the loads. They spent almost as much time shoveling the wagon out as they did cutting wood.

Gary built a sled of sorts, more like a large toboggan that they had to drag, themselves after the snow became too deep for the horses to manage. The men grumbled and complained and refused to cut more wood. After spending a cold night without a fire, they cut wood again.

Winter lasts a very long time in Interior Alaska and by spring, no one was in a very good mood. A lot of the mine owners had left when winter started and several of their workers went with them. There wasn't much for them to do when everything they were used to doing was frozen solid. Some returned to Seattle or whatever area they originated from and others spent the winter along the coast or on the islands in Southeastern Alaska. They could fish and hunt all winter and there were saloons and assorted other forms of entertainment to entice them to spend their money. Many that remained in Paradise swore they were going "Outside" next winter. No way were they going to ever spend another winter with nothing to do.

Two that had not left were Gale and Reggie. Everyone wished they had. What Reggie didn't think of, Gale did and the two made themselves very unpopular. They had taken enough sugar from the wagons while they were unloaded at Luke's to make some sort of alcohol. They called it beer, but it had berries, potatoes, corn meal and anything else they thought might ferment and add to the kick. They didn't know where Josh had gone, but figured he would be back and they would be here to greet him. He usually thought up ideas to earn them money without their having to work too hard for it.

Reggie was still smarting from the public humiliation of being refused by Mattie. Just who did she think she was, anyway? She was no beauty like those other women. She should be grateful he was offering marriage. He still had small red scars from that other woman's whip. The scars were fading, but the memories were fresh and burned into his mind. He and Gale pondered ways and means of getting even. Gale didn't have much actual experience with any of the women, but he was good at imagining the slights suffered by Reggie and Reggie was his friend.

Chapter 14

Temperance, Jasmine, Pearl and Sue Lee started walking down to the Laundry every day to get some exercise and outdoor air as the days started getting longer after the New Year.

They found that they felt much better and were not so irritable after their excursions. Charity and Mattie welcomed the break and they usually all shared lunch.

They had noticed Reggie and Gale watching them as they walked through town each day but as the only women in town, they were getting used to having men watch them. However, Reggie and Gale didn't look at them as the other men did. Most of the men were very polite and offered assistance. The other two just stared and glared.

Sue Lee wanted to see what all was left in the store, she wanted to purchase some cloth to make some dish towels for the house. She dashed across the street, telling the others she would meet them later, at the Laundry.

The two men decided this was too good to pass up and waylaid her before she reached the store. One threw a coat over her head as the other grabbed her around the arms to pull her back into a small dim alley.

The shock of being grabbed immobilized Sue Lee for a few seconds, then the men thought they had grabbed a wild cat by mistake. She was kicking, hitting, scratching and cursing them in two languages. The men were getting in each other's way more than they were making progress in subduing her. The coat did muffle her screams, but her feet were doing real damage to the ones trying to hold her.

As Mitch walked by the alley on his way to his office, he heard a scuffle going on in the alley. Curiosity and boredom turned his steps down the dark little alley and he soon made out the struggling shape between two larger shapes. Two against one never did seem all that fair and Mitch prided himself on being a fair man.

He pulled one man away from the melee and found Reggie dangling from his grip. That was never a good sign, so he punched him to keep him quiet and yanked the other one loose from the cloaked figure still screaming in the folds of the coat. He popped that one on the chin also and soon had a fighting mad Sue Lee freed of the coat.

She immediately attacked her two attackers and proceeded to inflict a bit of damage before he got her settled down.

The noise brought a few more curious men into the alley and they soon had Gale and Reggie frog marching toward the improvised jail in the outhouse hole.

Diego yelled at them for throwing the smelly duo into their fairly clean holding tank. It was fairly obvious they were strangers to soap and water during the winter

132

months. The hole was going to be fairly crowded if any more miscreants were included in the population living there. Mitch told Diego now there were two more helpers on cutting wood and shoveling snow around town. Diego grumbled but the thought of someone else doing the cutting of wood cheered him up.

Diego was fairly fastidious and as soon as the others left, he advanced on the two new residents. He proceeded to tell them that they would clean up before evening as he was not going to try sleeping in a room that smelled like the outhouse was already in production.

Once they were cleaned up a bit, he asked what they were in for. Gale told him they tried to grab one of those girls parading around town. They picked the littlest one as they thought she would be easy to subdue and she was away from the rest of the flock. They sounded like a flock of birds twittering down the street as they walked.

Diego told them the dark haired one was his and they said there were four dark haired ones, which one did he claim? He thought a moment then told them the one that was married to the gringo. They immediately knew which one he meant. Reggie said he had a prior gripe with her, she had used that whip on him and he still carried scars. Diego stopped and thought a few minutes. Maybe one of the other girls would do just as well. He really would rather not be bothered with a husband trying to get his wife back, but then he thought of the debt her father owed him. She was his, no matter if she was married. The fact that she looked down her nose at him would make his revenge even better. He would keep her a while, just so she knew who was boss, then sell her to one of the slave traders along the coast. She might even end up in some harem somewhere. The thought of that brought a smile to his face. It would be a perfect ending to his waiting all these years to claim her. The fact that he had cheated to win her made no difference. She was his.

The men spent all their time that they were not out working, planning and then planning some more on how they were going to get loose and carry out the plans they were making for the women.

Diego found willing confederates in Reggie and Gale. Neither had any scruples and no problem with the thought of kidnapping the women. One of the men that had traveled up with him refused to participate. The other two were indifferent. They didn't really care one way or the other.

Diego, Reggie and Gale spent their evenings planning and re-planning their ultimate revenge. They wanted to make it so perfect no one would ever catch them. They knew if they were caught, it would be a death sentence, one way or another. Frontier justice was usually swift and unforgiving.

Reggie and Gale became so enthralled with the idea of what they were going to do that they were practically giddy with the suppressed excitement while they worked, during the day. The men chosen to guard them while they worked knew they had to be hatching some nefarious scheme, but had not caught on to them teaming up with Diego as he was barely civil to anyone. Jose was pulled from the wood cutting and given quarters in the back of the Laundry. He liked keeping the fire going at night and helped Mattie during the day. He really liked not being bullied around by the other men in the hole. They thought he was too simple to understand any of the plans they were making so talked fairly freely around him.

Not long after he started staying at the Laundry, he was helping Charity wring out clothes and told her part of the plan Diego was dreaming up for Temperance. He liked Temperance and all the women. They were all kind to him and treated him very well, although once in a while more like a younger brother. Mattie would prepare meals but the women always brought lunch down for Charity and enough to share for him and Mattie, also.

Now they talked about how to protect themselves against Diego, Gale and Reggie. Jose taught them some knife defense and Mattie set up a target for them to practice against. Sue Lee taught them all some hand to hand defense. Jose was surprised the first time she knocked him down using her feet. She weighed about half as much as he did. Then she threw him over her shoulder and he looked up at her in wonder. He was always afraid he would hurt them so was not a very good practice dummy for their throws, but he gave them confidence that they could actually do it.

Winter progressed and finally the snow started evaporating. There was no dripping or running water yet, just the snow pack slowly loosing mass and around the trees, bits of bare ground could now be seen. There were still deep drifts and down in some valleys, the snow looked like it was there to stay. The calendar might claim it was now springtime, but anyone looking out the window would say it was still winter. The sun did have some warmth to it now but in the shade, it was still below freezing.

The little marten that had been coming around the house eating the scraps of bread and meat left out for the jays stopped coming around and the women hoped that was because it moved on, not that someone trapped it. They had not heard of anyone trapping around town, but it was possible.

The women were finally getting comfortable using snowshoes. They hoped it was a skill that once learned, always remembered. They were taking short jaunts up the hill behind the house and checking out the dam on the creek above town. Water would show up on top the ice and snow, then freeze and then appear again. Gary told them that was called glaciering, here. The entire valley above the dam was full of ice. They wondered how it ever had time to thaw enough for mining and use by the town in the short summers.

They had noticed there was almost no darkness at night, now and were prepared this year. Each of the bedrooms had room darkening curtains. It might not make the rooms entirely dark, but certainly darker than it was without them.

Temperance thought she might be with child by the time most of the snow was gone. She finally asked Mattie about it.

"Lordy, I don't have a clue. My Mister died in a fight over in Dawson, we had just got married and we never had any little ones." Mattie told her.

Charity told her she never had any, but she was the oldest of a very large family and had been around her Ma when she was in the family way. She had helped the midwife when her younger siblings were born. She guessed they would know for sure in a few more months.

"Gee, thanks a lot. In a few months, I will look like a whale. Or not," and she collapsed laughing on a bench near the door.

The streets were a sea of mud and the raised boardwalks helped along the store fronts, but trying to cross the street from block to block was nearly impossible. The women stopped making their daily treks to the Laundry. Charity and Mattie set up private space inside the large building and stayed there until the ground firmed up again. Jose ran errands for them and brought in all the wood needed for the fires.

As the snow melted away from the house and yard, Temperance decided to plant all the remaining shriveled sprouting potatoes and onions left in the cellar. There was a fairly large flat area that got full sunlight in summer and was slightly protected from winds by the house and woodshed. She and the other women started clearing scrub brush and dried weeds from the ground as soon as it was bare of snow.

Jose came up and said Mattie sent him to spade up a garden for them. The ground was still too frozen, so he helped them scatter ashes from the stoves over the area and some of the barn litter from the horses.

He told them they could plant some of the beans if they soaked them overnight first, after the frosts quit. Pearl had

137

saved seeds from some winter squash they used during the winter. They would actually have a fairly good garden.

Men were returning to town from their winter Outside or along the river. Travel was easier by dog team and most took advantage of that.

Fernando went from ridiculing the women's efforts at gardening to an interest in how to make it work. He told them of the glass houses used in Europe to grow delicate flowers and exotic fruits in climates not suited , even going so far as to draw up plans. Gary came by and soon the two were planning a glass growing house in one corner of the garden. The squash would do better in it than outdoors at the mercy of the weather. Some of the garlic cloves and seeds from the chili peppers in the food supplies from the wagon he was brought up on should grow in it, also.

Before all the snow was gone, a glass growing house was already built in one corner by the garden. The growing benches were constructed, then filled with the used litter from the horse barn. Buckets of dirt were brought up from the cellar, enlarging the cellar and providing thawed dirt to plant the squash and pepper seeds. A trellis was built along the north wall and soaked bean seeds planted along the trellis with the squash in front. The beans could climb above the squash. The trellis took the place of corn as they had no corn to plant. The horse manure under the dirt warmed the soil and kept the seeds from freezing out as they would have if planted outdoors. Corn, beans and squash traditionally were planted together by the Native people and continued to be grown that way for the best results. Garlic cloves were tucked here and there in the edges of the growing boxes.

Temperance wasn't used to seeing her Grandfather actually getting in and working. He was very good at supervising, but hands on work was beneath him. She was amazed to see him roll up his sleeves and helping on the greenhouse construction. To see him checking for the first growth, then inspecting daily was something she never expected to see. The day she found him watering plants once they emerged was a total shock. To the surprise of them both, she hugged him.

"Oh Grandfather, I do love you."

Then she fled back to the house. He stood there in stunned surprise, then a slow smile cracked his stern face. It didn't last long, but it had appeared.

Chapter 15

Josh hiked over the hill north of town and stopped to gaze at the activity below. He felt almost like he was returning home. Something about this small scruffy little town drew him. He set up camp on the hilltop. He was in no hurry to let anyone know he was back. Things had not worked out as he planned over the winter and he was at loose ends, now.

Working for someone else as a Gambler in Nome was not the way to make a grubstake. When he had a time escaping a planned necktie party with him as the main attraction meant he lost all he planned on bringing back inland with him. Luck showed up again, when he reached the Yukon and found several teams of dogs waiting for the drovers that were supposed to bring the freight upriver that was already loaded on the large freight sleds.

He hired on as a driver and brought the load on the river as far as Rampart, then hiked overland from there. Staying to the ridge tops, he bypassed the worst drifts and made fairly good time arriving at Paradise.

Now he sat there, looking at the bustling little town almost as broke as when he left. Laughter drifted up the hill from the large house nearest him. Evidently the people had

141

not frozen out over the winter as he had predicted. Maybe the sawdust in the double thick walls really did work.

As he sat there, the hairs on the back of his neck started prickling. He slowly turned his head and found himself face to face with a large bear, just freshly emerged from hibernation. It was definitely an 'Oh Shit' moment.

They stared at each other for a lifetime, he thought, when a small sound behind the bear caused it to turn its' head and suddenly turn and walked toward the sound. A very small cub tumbled out of the brush, followed by another. The bear plopped down and the cubs pushed to begin nursing.

Josh scrambled to his feet as the bear turned her back, grabbed his pack and rifle, forgot his coat and backed as quickly as he could away from the area. When the bear was totally out of sight, he turned and ran a while. When he finally stopped, leaned against a tree and caught his breath, he found that he was now at the other end of town and slowly began heading down the steep hill to walk back up the road leading to town.

Gale saw him first. He and Reggie were trudging with the rest of the crew back to their jail quarters. No one knew what to do with the prisoners and they certainly didn't want to just turn them loose in town to be a problem, yet again.

Gale nudged Reggie and pointed his chin in Josh's direction. Reggie asked him if he had something wrong with his jaw. Gale jerked his head toward Josh. Reggie yelled for the guard to come help Gale, he was having some sort of attack. Gale whacked Reggie and Reggie whacked him back.

"Hey, I don't want to get whatever you have. It might be something contagious, like hydrophobia or measles. Don't you be touching or biting me." Reggie pushed away from Gale.

"Josh, you idiot. Josh is over there by those trees."

"Well dang, why didn't you just say so, instead of twitching and scaring me," Reggie mumbled.

By now everyone was looking over under the trees and Josh was trying to make himself invisible. He might have succeeded better if he hadn't stumbled into a hole near a tree that someone had dug, checking for gold.

Damn, just what he needed, two idiots for confederates. Now he wished he had just stayed still instead of trying to let them know he was back. He wondered why they were under guard now that he looked a little closer at the group still carrying axes and saws. He never knew Gale or Reggie to do an honest day's work in all the time he had known either of them.

He found the cabin he used last year and it appeared abandoned, so he moved right in. Of course there was no wood as he had not left any last autumn when he left. After scouting around in the trees behind the cabin, he found enough dry wood to start a small fire. He did find part of a bag of dry beans on a shelf, so started a pot of beans cooking, even though they would take hours. Oh well, he had nothing but time.

One of the guards on the work detail from the jail let Mitch know that Josh was back in the area. Mitch walked over to the Laundry and told Charity. She and Mattie were finishing up the day's wash. Folding and placing each order

143

of clothes in a separate pile, waiting for the owners to come pick them up.

Mitch offered to walk Charity home. He felt unsettled that Josh was back and they still had no way of proving whether he had anything to do with the body found up in the berry patch or not.

The jacket looked like the one Josh always wore, but there were many of those coats in Alaska. The timing of his leaving town seemed incriminating but could be just coincidence, maybe. There were just no hard facts, like an eye witness.

Josh kept a low profile, trying to figure out just why he even bothered to return to this stiff necked town. As gold strikes went, it wasn't even one of the big ones. Yes, there was money here. It seemed that all the rich claims were already filed and working. No one really knew if the winter's workings would prove the ground still rich enough to continue. Some of the claims on deeper ground did keep a crew working during the winter, drift mining underground.

The men built up a fire on the frozen ground and let it burn overnight. Then, they would dig out the thawed muck and stockpile it to sluice the coming summer after it all thawed again. It was hard dirty work and not for the likes of him. That would be even harder labor than staying on his father's farm in Poland and working himself to death. He was intended for finer things.

Josh had worked as a packer for a wealthy young man from Europe one summer. They had become friends of a sort and Josh liked to imagine himself living in the splendor

144

the young man took for granted at home. He could only imagine eating from fine china with utensils made of real silver or gold, servants waiting on him and soft clothing against his skin.

He had seen Nobles riding in fine carriages before his family immigrated to America. He knew what it felt like to have to bow down when the Overlord came to collect his portion of the harvest. He wanted to BE the Overlord. If he made enough money here, he could go back and buy his way to the upper class. If he were very wealthy, he could marry one of their daughters and gain immediate entrance to their ranks.

Damn Ilena for not following his orders. Now everything was a mess and he didn't know how he would be able to recover the papers she had carried.

While Josh sat and stewed, Reggie and Gale planned ways to escape their imprisonment. Diego wanted out, also, so soon joined in their discussions on ways and means. The others would go along with anything Diego wanted to do. At least at present, they had regular meals and a warm place to sleep. They were not complaining too much except about the work. None of them enjoyed that. If they liked work, they would have steady jobs.

Chapter 16

Temperance was fairly certain she was in the family way, now. She was feeling ill every morning, which Charity told her was normal. She wanted to nap at odd hours throughout the day and was ready for bed right after the evening meal.

She had not told Luke yet. She figured there was still plenty of time just in case she was wrong. The trees were leafing out and everything was bursting out in bloom. While she, Pearl, Jasmine and Sue Lee were walking through the woods, searching for more plants to add to the yard, they saw a cow moose with a very new calf and stood still, just watching the calf take trembling steps.

All were unaware of Josh, standing back in the deep shadows of a stand of spruce. He watched Temperance with especial interest. She had dared use her whip on him. He had a score to settle with her and would take pleasure in giving her intense pain. He wasn't sure how to achieve those ends, but would be thinking about it.

That evening, he sat close to the back of the building the prisoners were kept in.

"Gale, Reggie, can you hear me?"

Reggie perked up at the sound of a voice from outside, calling to him and Gale.

"We are right here. What do you want?" Reggie answered.

"How about I get you out of there and we head somewhere a bit better suited to our likes?"

"Josh, I knew you would come rescue us. How you going to get us out of here?"

"Don't worry, it might take me a couple of days, but I will get you out and we can figure out where to go from there," Josh told him.

The next morning the Guard taking them out to cut firewood was surprised to find the men in jovial moods and no whining and complaining during the day of work. The next day was the same and the Guard relaxed a bit, thinking maybe the improved weather made everyone in better spirits. It was a bad mistake.

An arm came around him from behind and a conk on the head silenced him. His hand convulsively tightened his grasp on the shotgun he carried and it went off, striking one of Diego's cohorts dead center and a few stray pellets hitting the other one where they had been standing beside Diego.

"Oops, sorry about that. I do hope he wasn't important to you. The other one should make it with some medical assistance." Josh told Diego.

"It's not important. They were just available when I needed them and they did not perform all that well. Thank you for setting me free. I have a few scores to settle and then I shall return home."

"We have some to settle around here, also, but I am thinking maybe we should move out for a while and come back when no one is expecting us. You can come along or not, no matter," Josh told him.

"I suggest we discuss this somewhere far from here as that shot will soon have others coming to see what the problem is. Others in town always know where this crew is during the day." Diego said.

The injured man lay quietly on the ground, hoping they would forget about him. He closed his eyes and slowed his breathing as much as possible. That Diego. He had always been a faithful friend and helped out whenever he could, why was Diego leaving him now?

The men spared little thought to the bodies lying on the ground around them, only taking the time to take the weapons and everything in the pockets of the Guard. There were a few coins and Josh pocketed them.

"You'll have to ride double with Reggie as he is the smallest one of us, I wasn't planning on spares and no other horses were available at the moment." Josh told Diego.

"Hey, that is my horse anyway. So are the other two. I brought them up from California when we came up this winter."

"Oops, well, they were the easiest horses to get to. They might not be missed quite as soon as any others in town, not that there are all that many in town, anyway." Josh said.

After the men rode off, Antonio raised himself on one arm and looked at his dead and injured companions. He eased the ax out from under Juan and scooted over to a small tree. It was difficult cutting while sitting on the ground, but he didn't have a lot of choices. At least the snow was gone now and he should be able to hobble back to town and let people know what had happened out here. He had no animosity for the Guard. The man had always been fair with them and brought extras once in a while to give them a treat at lunch time even. Juan had been a companion over the years and they didn't fight or argue. He would miss him, and thought he deserved better than Diego had dismissed them as both just useful tools. Well, if possible, he would help see Senor Diego got what was coming to him, and those others, also.

As he hobbled out of the trees, on his improvised crutch, he met several of the men from town coming up the hill.

Luke and Mitch were among the first to reach him.

"What happened? We heard a shot." Luke asked.

"Senor, someone hit the Guard. Juan and I were shot when his shotgun went off. Juan is dead, I think, but the others left with the man that hit the Guard. They have three horses from the ones that came with the old man."

"Wait here and we will help you on down the hill. We will bring the bodies back with us."

Antonio continued to hobble slowly down the hill, he could do it, if he took his time. He soon heard the men coming back down the hill behind him. He slowed even more and stopped, leaning against a tree.

He told them to go on ahead, he would catch up with them. He wasn't badly hurt, it was just painful and he would stop and see if the new doctor that was setting up was ready for a patient. Town had been very dull as far as patients for the doctor went, as most of the rowdier folk

150

were gone all winter. Now that they were trickling back in, maybe he would be busy enough to actually stay. The last one left from boredom.

When Antonio hobbled into his office, the doctor was reading a book, with his feet up on the table, leaned back in his chair and almost asleep. He was so surprised to see an actual patient that he fell trying to get up and Antonio ended up helping him get back on his feet.

"My first real patient. You are actually hurt or sick, aren't you?"

"Yes, I have some shotgun pellets in my leg. I can come back later if you are busy."

They both laughed about that and the doctor soon had Antonio sitting on the table and was picking out the pellets. When he had the pellets out and the leg was bandaged up, he told Antonio he was going to have to take it easy a few days.

"I don't think that is going to be a problem, the rest of the crew are missing or dead."

Luke and Mitch came in the door just as Antonio said that and they looked at each other. Yes, just what were they going to do about Antonio? They knew he wasn't the one responsible although he had gone along and didn't try to stop any of the actions of Diego. They thought he probably had served enough time in the makeshift jail to cover his crimes. The doctor looked the Guard over and told him to watch for dizziness.

"Do you know anything about carpentry?" Luke asked him.

151

"Yes, my father was a carpenter and I used to work with him until I got involved with Diego. Papa said he would be the death of me, but I was too stupid to know he was right."

"Do you want a regular job? That outhouse needs to be completed and I doubt if you really want to spend any more time in it until it is completed unless it is just to work on it."

"Certainly, tell me what you want done and I can do it, I actually like building and might go home and tell my Papa so."

They walked slowly over to the outhouse/jail. Luke described how he wanted it finished for a multihole public outhouse with privacy stalls on each side. One side for ladies, one side for men. He did not want the indiscriminate use of alleyways and the edge of the woods around town to create a health problem nor an odor problem now that summer might finally be here. He had read some radical new theories about cleanliness contributing to better health. He also didn't want his town to stink.

Flies and assorted other bugs were plentiful enough without giving them more places to multiply. He was filling in all the bog holes right around town to help cut down on the mosquitoes and pouring a bit of oil on top of a few of them seemed to be helping, also. He didn't think there were as many this year as there were last year.

"You will need a place to stay, now, so until we can find something, you are welcome to sleep in my barn or the grain shed as long as you don't smoke in either one. I'm afraid of having the place go up in smoke. I wish now that I had brought up brick to build with, but wasn't sure how it would do up here. Maybe native stone would have been better."

"What you have seems to be fairly warm for such a large house. I haven't seen anything like it since I got here." Antonio told him.

"I figured if I wanted a gently raised lady to come live here and be happy, I better at least have a nice house for her. Not some 8 x 10 foot hovel. So far, she seems happy with the house and didn't freeze to death like everyone told her she would."

Antonio grinned at him, "That's always a good start."

The man might not pick the best people to hang out with, but at least he had a sense of humor, Luke thought. Maybe he just never had opportunity before to travel a different trail. He would treat him as any other until he proved otherwise.

Temperance still had not told Luke what she suspected. She thought she might just be getting fat from not being as active as she had always been back in California. She was used to riding most of each day and helping with the cattle. This being a lady all the time was not her preferred way to live. None of the other women enjoyed riding so she started dressing in her boots and breeches and taking her horse out for a run every day. The pants were getting so tight, she figured she better start eating less of all the good food Pearl, Jasmine and Sue Lee prepared every day. She really should learn to cook. One of these days it might be necessary if the other women found other work to do that they liked better or got married.

She was riding a bit farther from the house than she usually rode when she heard the sound of another horse off in the distance. She paid little attention to the sound until it became obvious the other rider was paralleling her route and drawing closer in a manner that almost seemed stealthy.

As she glanced around, she realized the rider was subtly edging her farther and farther away from the well-used trail and onto another barely discernable one through thicker vegetation. She slowly started turning her horse on around until she was heading back toward town.

Then she heard another rider coming in from her other side. She kicked her heels into her horse and yelled. The horse was willing and they broke out of the trees above town, riding like the hoyden her Grandfather claimed she was. She slowed only as she neared the house and was so glad to see Luke coming out the door that she almost flung herself onto him from the back of her barely stopped horse.

"Whoa, what's wrong? Are you okay?" he asked as he held her close.

She was trembling so bad it took her a few seconds to find her voice.

"Someone tried to catch me, in the woods. There was only one at first, but when I saw I was being maneuvered onto another trail, I turned to head back and another one came from the other side. They didn't say anything and I didn't hear any shots, but they scared me."

She finally ran out of steam and realized how silly she sounded. She shrugged out of his arms and stood back, pushing her hair back under her hat, glad she had the chin strap on or she would have lost it in her mad dash for home. By now she was starting to feel embarrassed by her panic.

"I'm sorry, I over reacted, I think," she said.

"No, I think you did the right thing. Usually when a person feels threatened, they are correct. I would rather have you gallop in here any time and you are certainly welcome to jump on me any time you feel like it. I rather liked it," he smiled and saw her relax a little bit and a tentative smile touched her lovely mouth.

"So you really don't mind if I jump on you now and then? Let's see how well you like it when I am as big as a house in a few more months," she told him with lowered lashes.

He stood there in stunned silence a couple of moments, then whooped. "Are you trying to tell me we are going to have a baby?"

"Shhhh, not so loud, everyone will hear you. Nice people don't talk about such things," she reminded him.

"Nice people be hanged, I want the world to know we are going to have a little one. Are you feeling okay? Is this why you no longer come down for breakfast and stay upstairs until breakfast is over in the mornings? Should you be out riding? Are you sure you are okay?"

"Husband, if you hush up a second, I will try to answer all those questions. I feel fine now. Yes, that is why I have been waiting until later for breakfast. I have rode horses since I was a baby myself. A little riding isn't going to hurt me now. I am just fine. There, did I get them all?" she answered.

Luke smiled at his adorable wife and kissed her soundly.

"Luke that is no way to behave in public. However, if you feel like an afternoon nap, I am sure we could be more comfortable in our room, hmmm?"

Chapter 17

When they emerged from their room some time later, they both looked refreshed and well kissed.

"So you and Luke are taking afternoon naps now?" asked Jasmine.

"Yes, I told him about the baby and he was afraid I've been overdoing it." Temperance tried to keep a straight face but failed. She burst out laughing and the other women joined her.

"You certainly sleep very noisily, the baby will have a hard time sleeping through that after he is here." Pearl teased her.

"He? The baby is a boy?" Temperance asked her.

"I think so. I am not positive, but he feels like a boy to me," she answered. "It is probably best not to tell Luke in case I am wrong."

"Alright, but how can you tell?" Temperance asked.

"I really don't know, but usually I am right," Pearl answered.

"I wonder if the store has any flannel so I can start making baby clothes and diapers."

"I think there is some over under all the other bolts of fabric. It isn't something this town of men have a lot of need for," Jasmine teased.

"Let's go down in the morning and see. Maybe we can all start sewing so time will go faster. Do any of you know what we need or how to make them?"

Charity said she probably could remember once she got started after helping her mother with so many younger ones before she left home.

The next morning all the women walked down the hill with Charity on her way to work. They left early enough to stop at the store and see if there was any flannel in stock.

The store keeper wasn't sure what to think of the 5 women coming in his store together. When they asked about flannel, he was about dying of curiosity. It would be very poor manners to inquire as to what use they needed it for as so many things unmentionable in mixed company could account for its use.

Besides baby clothes, many ladies made personal clothes out of flannel and some even made pantaloons out of it for the colder weather. Besides the reusable clothes used in the tending to everyday bodily functions, there were the monthly uses ladies had for absorbent clothes. He blushed even thinking about what its probable use would be and determined to do his best not to say anything about it at all, ever. He wished he had a wife so she could tend to the ladies' purchases.

As the clerk tallied up her purchases, Temperance wondered about his blushes and stammers. The poor man was embarrassed so badly he was barely coherent. She hoped they had purchased enough that they wouldn't have to subject the poor man to any more purchases of something that so obviously distressed him.

159

They continued on to the Laundry with Charity and she helped them decide what size diapers should be. Then she cut out the tiniest little gown any of them had ever seen.

"Now use this as a pattern and cut them all this size. Then sew around the side seams, then turn it and fold the seam over so there are no raw edges to damage delicate new skin and sew it again like this," she demonstrated.

"My mother called that a French seam and I had to make sure it tucked in well so the flannel doesn't ravel and so there are no rough edges. New babies have tender skin. Once you have the gown sewn together, then crochet a soft edging all around all the openings to finish them and make ties at the neck to hold it closed when the baby is wearing it." Charity continued her lesson.

The other four women and Mattie paid close attention. Then a customer came in and Mattie waited on him. After he left, she asked Charity if she ever considered sewing to make a living.

"No, I love to sew but have never even thought about charging others for it."

"Why don't we add sewing shirts for the Miners as another means of making some money? You could still work in here and whenever there was spare time, we could sew shirts. I have a sewing machine in my living quarters that will make short work of doing all the long hems on those diapers and also on shirts so we could turn them out fairly fast"

"You have a sewing machine? I have never used one and my mother always wanted one. I can do the hand sewing and you can do the machine?"

"No, I will teach you how to use the machine. Since I hurt my hip when I fell, my leg doesn't do too well on the treadle and I haven't been able to keep caught up as well on the mending and such."

Temperance and the other women were practically jumping up and down in excitement, "May we learn, too?"

"No time like the present, while we have a slow day. Maybe the lot of us can move the machine out here where we can wait on customers and sew in between." Mattie told her.

The women soon had the sewing machine set up behind the counter Mattie had in the front to wait on customers. She soon had them sewing hems on diapers. She told them there wasn't too much that could go wrong on a diaper. As long as the pins held and it was changed often, it would do its job whether the hem was straight or meandered a bit.

With all the sadirons always heating on the stove and the ironing board so handy, the hems were ironed flat before attempting to sew them and the tiny gowns were then tried, the same way. Sewing the seams after ironing them flat made it so much easier to make a French seam. By the time they stopped for lunch, they had an impressive amount of small clothing made for the future heir to the town. The edges still needed to be crocheted, but they had months to manage that.

Mitch came in the Laundry while they were eating lunch and looked over the sewing machine and the piles of cloth laying all over the available work surfaces.

"Would you be in the market to make some work shirts for me?" he asked.

Charity came over and asked him what types of fabric he wanted and how soon he would need them. She told him if he supplied the material, he could go pick out exactly what he wanted and then she could give him a price and take measurements.

He soon returned with the amount of fabric she told him would be needed for a shirt and took his measurements. He told her the style shirt he wanted for a work shirt. He liked the pullover style favored by the railroad workers so were called railroad shirts. They had eyelets up an opening at the neck that closed with laces. He wanted the tails long enough that they wouldn't ride up if he was working hard and get his middle bitten by bugs. The fabric was a lightweight canvas, pretty much bug proof for being bitten.

With the sewing machine, it would be simple to sew as she would not be ruining her fingers pushing a needle through the tough fabric. After she was a partner here, she would be saving her money to buy a sewing machine for herself. Temperance wanted one for up at the house. She had immediately decided it was her new favorite household appliance, right up there with the gas lights Luke was installing in the house.

Hand sewing was never her favored chore and the nuns at school used it as a form of punishment as they knew she was truly being punished if she had to sit indoors and sew by hand while everyone else was outdoors. She would have to ask Luke if it were possible to get a sewing machine.

She had lingered behind, learning all she could about the sewing machine and was not paying attention while she walked home. It was not dark, so she was totally unprepared when strong arms reached out from an alleyway and grabbed her. Before she got more than a squeak out, a rag was shoved in her mouth and a sack tied over her head, her hands yanked behind her and tied. Then she was stuffed down into a large bag similar to the ones used for laundry from the mines and dropped into the back of a wagon, waiting at the other end of the alley.

Fear coursed through her but she was determined no one would ever see it. She was quite limber and soon managed to scoot herself through the loop her tied hands made behind her back. After some of the situations her brothers loved to pull on her, this was almost easy. Her long skirts were the worst impediment. Once she managed to get them in front, she worked at getting the rag out of her mouth. She still had bouts of nausea and resolved to not end up choking just because someone wanted her to feel helpless.

Once the rag was out of her mouth and she could breathe deeply, she assessed her situation. No one knew she was missing yet. The women at the house thought she was taking longer than planned at the Laundry. Mattie and Charity thought she had headed for home. She chewed on the thongs holding her wrists together and found her contortions getting her hands up front had stretched them a bit and she didn't have to chew through them as she feared. She pulled with her teeth and soon had one hand free and just left the thong looped around the other for the

163

present. She didn't know how long she had until they stopped to check on their prize.

She reached under her skirts and pulled out the small revolver Luke had given her a while back. She kept it in a fitted holster on her thigh. The knife beside it was pulled out so she now had a weapon in each hand.

The knife was razor sharp so she had no trouble slitting the bag she was bundled into. Slowly, she inched her way out, expecting someone to notice that their victim had been very active since being dropped into the back of the wagon.

She heard low voices discussing something and it sounded like one did not agree with what they were supposed to do next. She slowly eased to the back of the wagon and over the tailgate. She slowly dropped over the back of the wagon and took off as though the hounds of hell were on her tail. As she raced through the woods, she was just blindly running the opposite direction as the wagon was traveling, at first. Then she started paying some attention to where she was going.

She recognized an oddly shaped tree to her left and immediately veered around it and sped on down the hill toward the back of her home. She ran into Luke at full speed as she rounded the corner of the barn, knocking them both flat on the ground.

"Luke, get some men and horses and get up to the trail we went riding on last week. Some men kidnapped me and are in a wagon heading out that trail. If you hurry, you might catch them before they notice I am gone."

She tore on into the house, asked Jasmine to get her horse saddled please and then on to her room. She changed into

164

her riding gear. This was going to stop, now. She grabbed her whip and the larger shotgun and hand gun Luke gave her for bear protection and was back out the door before anyone in the house knew what was happening. The man coming out of the barn leading her horse barely had time to toss her the reins and she was up and gone. She hoped Luke was ahead of her, but if he wasn't, she could still make sure they were stalled long enough to catch up.

She almost ran over Reggie as she came around the odd shaped tree. He jumped back and gave a startled yelp. Gale rushed out of the trees on the other side of the wagon trail and made a grab for her horse's reins. She smashed the whip handle down into his face, breaking his nose and whirled the horse around in time to catch Reggie off guard and popped him with the whip.

"Did you catch the troublesome witch?" a voice called out from the trail behind her and she whirled the horse around yet again to face the unknown person coming down the trail from where the wagon was parked.

Josh and Diego rode around the clump of trees and she was so surprised she just stared a couple of seconds. Then she charged. Her horse responded beautifully to the knee pressure and jumped right into the two horses facing her. She slashed with the knife in one hand as she whirled the whip in the other, scoring bloody but nonlethal hits with each.

The horse turned and now she pulled up the shotgun. It loosely covered all four men. Gale clutched his broken nose, Reggie held his bleeding neck and Diego clutched the slashed arm she had scored with her knife. Josh held his

165

arm, also and watched in dull surprise as the trail the lash had left slowly started to bleed.

Josh thought she certainly didn't learn that at the school run by nuns near her Grandfather's ranch. But then Diego had said she spent most of her time running wild with her brothers.

The sound of more horses and men came through the brush and trees. Soon Luke, Mitch and a couple of other men rode into her view.

"How the devil did you beat us up here? How am I supposed to rescue you if you persist in rescuing yourself?" Luke asked her.

"I was afraid they would get away and there would be no proof they kidnapped me. I refuse to let them dictate where I go or where I ride. Do you have enough rope to just hang them right here? I have some, but only enough to hang them one at a time."

Josh had been slowly edging his horse back as the others talked and now he whirled it around and took off at a gallop. He had seen hangings before and even helped in a few and did not want to be the main attraction at one today. Diego took advantage of the distraction to kick his horse into a gallop right through the middle of the group in front of him and was soon out of sight, also.

Reggie and Gale were on foot and no way could they even consider making a getaway. Not that they didn't think about it, but if the murderous look in Temperance's eye was any indication, they would be extremely foolhardy to even attempt it on foot. Then they looked at Luke and almost passed out. He looked even more murderous than his wife.

"Well, I catch them by myself, then the posse shows up and half the prisoners get away? If I were the insecure type, I would be wondering which side you all were on just about now," she turned her horse and started back to the house.

Still smarting from Temperance's little speech, the men recovered the wagon and brought the sorry remaining kidnappers back to town.

Reggie and Gale could not believe what had just happened. They were mostly the helpers, they had not really wanted to be part of this mess. Now they were going back to the makeshift jail while the others went free. All they ever wanted was some girls to earn them a living in their very own saloon. What was so bad about that?

First, Doc, the only one of the three with any money went and got himself killed and they lose all chance of seeing their dream come to life. Then when they tried to brazen their way into making it come true, people just had to keep expecting them to actually work or pay their way. This was just so unfair. Then they found that their jail was now halfway enclosed for its original use and yet they were going to be put back down in the other half until someone could figure out what to do with them. Reggie wanted to cry. He wasn't going to get his saloon, Mattie definitely was not going to marry him and there were no pretty biddable girls to earn him a good living. How could his simple dream have turned into such a nightmare?

Gale had his fill of this whining little man. He was promised an easy way to make a good living and all he had

167

to show for it was painful bruises and a broken nose. Now he was stuck down here in this almost covered over outhouse hole. Work was a rotten four letter word yet he had been forced to work most of the winter at hard physical labor. Now here he was, back at their tender mercies yet again. He was too lazy to think up these kidnappings and thievery. He just followed along hoping he would never actually have to shoot someone or be expected to work for a living. He didn't mind intimidating folks with his size, and mean looks, but he preferred to let others do the actual work involved, even in breaking the Law. That Diego was one scary person and Josh wasn't any better. Just look at them. They were the ones wanting that snooty woman and they were both out there, free as birds and here he sat. So unfair.

Chapter 18

When Luke got home, he was not sure what kind of reception he was going to get from his wife. He certainly did not expect her to meet him at the door with a kiss and an apology.

"I am so sorry for saying such mean things, Luke. I was just so angry that they got away. I hate being afraid."

Luke melted. No matter what, he was going to keep her safe. If he had to hire every able bodied man in town to help watch for Diego and Josh, he would.

The next day Luke was sitting in Mitch's office, talking about ways to make sure the women were safe. Temperance seemed to be the main target but they remembered the attempt of one of the other girls, earlier. He asked Mitch what he thought about hiring watchmen to keep an eye on Temperance at all times.

"You really love that mean little woman, don't you? I never would have thought it of you. I expected you to come home with some blue blooded cold fish of a society girl and here you show up with one of the most fascinating, one of a kind women I have ever met, followed closely by that adorable redhead that is working with Mattie. Now that is some woman. If she would have me, I would marry that gal in a heartbeat." Mitch told him.

"Does she know how you feel?"

"I tried talking to her about it, but she won't listen to any serious talk. She says she isn't wife material. I consider her excellent wife material."

"She is worried about her past." Luke told him.

"It don't matter to me. I overheard her telling Mattie all about it before she started working there. She is honest, a hard worker and one of the nicest people I have ever met. As far as I am concerned, she is perfect." Mitch responded.

"Good luck on convincing her of all that. Temperance and I had a time convincing her to associate with us. She thought it would damage our reputations to be seen with her. I'll let Temperance know you would like to marry Charity and see if she can talk some sense into the woman. She usually has a lot of sense, but about that one subject, no, no way."

Later that night, Luke talked to Temperance about Mitch wanting to marry Charity. Temperance clapped her hands and laughed, "That would be so perfect. She would be a wonderful wife for Mitch. She already thinks he is just about perfect."

"That's funny, Mitch said the same thing about her."

The next morning the campaign was started to get Charity to see Mitch as a possible husband.

After a couple of days of being thrown in contact with Mitch on every pretext they could think of, Charity threw herself down on the bed and burst into tears.

"It's killing me to be around him all the time and not be able to think about having a lifetime of us being together. He is a most wonderful man and I love him. Would you

171

please stop asking me to deliver papers and meals to his office? I can't bear it.," she wailed.

"You do know he loves you and wants to marry you, don't you?"

"Once he knows about my past, he will be repulsed by me. No decent man is ever going to love me or want to marry me," she sniffled.

"Charity, listen to me. He has known about your past since the day you told Mattie. He was coming in when he heard you tell her before you started working there. He was afraid it would embarrass you to know he overheard so he went back out and then made more noise and came back in, remember?"

"Ye-e-es, I think I do. What if we got married, then someone came that knew about my past? He would be so humiliated and hurt. I couldn't bear it," she sobbed.

"I think you do him a great disservice, thinking he is so weak that anything others might think would damage him in some way. He seems to pretty much do and think as he pleases, from what I have seen. I think you need to talk to him. This is a chance for you to be happy and have your own family." Temperance told her.

Charity said she would think about it and went back downstairs to pick up her laundry.

As the women started for the Laundry the next morning, Temperance remembered a book she had promised to loan to Mattie and ran back indoors to get it. Charity continued on down the hill. Jasmine, Pearl and Sue Lee followed along a ways behind her, chattering among themselves. A man walking up the hill did a double take

172

and headed straight for Charity. He grabbed her arm and pulled her up short.

"Charity, just the person I was looking for. Doc told me if I ever made it up here, to stop on by and have a free one on the house."

Charity started to shrink back away from him. This man was responsible for the condition she found herself in, as an almost saloon girl.

The three young women walking behind finally noticed something was wrong, up ahead of them. They started hurrying to see if they could help when Temperance rounded the corner of the yard and saw Charity being held against her will. Suddenly there were four furies descending on the man and he didn't know just what hit him.

He finally broke away from the angry women and headed up the hill to get away from the crazed hellions. What was wrong with them? He just wanted some entertainment for the night? He was stumbling along cursing to himself when a small fuzzy animal dashed across the trail in front of him. He drew back his foot and kicked it hard. The startled squall of outrage was answered by a deep roar behind him.

His last thought was trying to make sense of what he was seeing, rearing up out of the tall brush under the trees. He looked up into the face of the outraged mother of the small cub he had kicked and then there was pain and darkness.

She did not bother with any mock charges and was not in the mood for a meal encased in troublesome material that caught in the teeth and caused assorted stomach problems. She dispatched him with speed and checked over her baby, still whimpering from his kick. She nuzzled her little one along the trail and left the area where a rude person treated a baby with such cruelty.

When the men rode up the trail a couple of hours later, they found the remains and determined he had not been fed on, then found tiny tracks of the cub and where he had kicked it, leaving soft downy fur on the toe of his boot and some on the trail.

"Anyone stupid enough to kick a cub is just committing suicide, as far as I can determine," Luke told the rest.

Several nodded in agreement. No one in their right mind would do something so stupid. The man either committed suicide by bear or was insane. They had enough problems of their own, they didn't need someone like that hanging around town.

The women watched the men bring the remains back for burial. They could not act sorry, but they did not celebrate, either, which Temperance claimed meant they really did have good manners anyway. Her Grandfather just shook his head and walked back into the house. She was never going to be a grand lady, but her husband seemed to love her, she was happy and not his problem. He smiled to himself and went on up to his room. It was time to plan his trip to see Europe once again. He might even stop in and see his grandsons at school. Nah, that was just too much to expect.

The man was buried with no ceremony although Luke did say a few words for his soul after he was buried. He figured the man needed it badly.

Temperance went to Charity's room and sat on her bed. Charity was darning a stocking and trying not to feel too happy that Jack was dead. She had loved him at one time, but being drugged and sold into slavery tended to kill those tender feelings for someone.

She knew if she had been wearing her hat with the long pins, she would have tried her best to do that deed herself. She was glad she did not do it, but could not muster up any feelings of sorrow so stayed in her room so she could control her emotions better. She was totally afraid she might yell out Yippee or something else unsuitable.

Temperance watched her darn for a few minutes, then suggested they go down to the Laundry and let Mattie in on all that had happened. Mattie probably already knew, but that didn't matter. Getting Charity out of her room and doing something to get her mind off it seemed a better idea.

While they walked, Charity talked about Jack a bit and then stopped and let out a yell. Then they continued walking.

"Feels better now, doesn't it?" Temperance asked her.

"Actually it does. I just hope no one noticed."

"Everyone is at work along the creeks or up in the hills somewhere. Even if someone did, you are entitled to let off a little steam now and then. Now you will never have to worry about this happening ever again. It is the perfect ending for him. No trial in the news, no gossip, and no worry he will show up ever again, anywhere"

By the time they reached the Laundry, Charity was feeling much better and even had a real smile on her face as she stepped through the door right into Mitch's arms.

175

Mitch caught her to help her keep her balance. Then he held on just a smidgeon too long before letting her go.

"Oh how I wish I could do that all the time," he murmured so only she could hear him. "You are so dear to me."

He tipped his hat and went on out the door. Charity stared after him.

"That man turns up everywhere," she muttered.

"That man is in love with you," Temperance told her.

"I just don't trust my ability to pick out a good man. Jack sort of spoiled things for me," she said.

"You seriously are not comparing Mitch to Jack, are you? Mitch has been a friend of Luke's since they were boys. I doubt if he would remain friends with someone like Jack." Temperance said.

"That does sound a bit silly, doesn't it? My head knows that, my heart is having trouble with it, just a little bit."

Mattie bustled over to see how they were doing. She had more orders for shirts and Charity started right in on filling the orders. Everyone liked the shirts she had made for Mitch. They helped prevent mosquito bites and took a long time and a lot of wear before wearing out. The narrow blue stripe on the white made them stand out and Temperance thought maybe she should make one for herself for when she could no longer get into her own clothes, even continuing tying strings on the sides and then across her tummy as she was doing now with her tight riding pants. If she made the shirt long enough, it would cover her bare belly.

Before they were ready to leave for home, Mitch stopped back over and offered to walk them home. He said there were some new people in town and he wanted to check them out before trusting them to not bother ladies walking alone.

Charity hated to admit it, but Mitch made her feel safe. She accepted his offer. Temperance was on one side of Charity and Mitch was on the other side as they came down the board walk in front of the General Store. Two strangers lounged in the chairs Nate kept outside for people to rest in. Temperance notice one had his hand under the paper across his lap and she caught the glint of a gun held in his lap under the paper. She loosened the coil of whip across her shoulder and in a low voice told Mitch they had trouble coming. He had not noticed the gun under the paper and smiled reassuringly at her. He was so happy to be walking Charity home he had forgotten the reason.

Temperance saw the other man stick out his foot for Mitch to trip over as the other one started to raise the gun in his lap.

Her whip snapped into him before he got the gun fully out from under the paper and she miscalculated a little bit on where she aimed. The man howled as he threw his gun and clutched himself.

Mitch saw the booted foot seconds before stumbling into it and reversed his step, pulling Charity back behind himself. The one curled in a fetal position on the boardwalk, clutching himself would not be a problem. Mitch and Temperance watched the other man. He started to put his hand in his coat and the whip wrapped around his arm,

177

yanking him off balance. The small hold out gun clattered onto the walk. Another man stepped out of the store and Temperance recognized him as one of the townsmen.

"I saw the whole thing. Any idea why they wanted to pick a fight with you or rather, try to gun you down in cold blood?" the man asked Mitch.

"I don't know any reasons right off hand. Maybe we can question these two and find out. I bet the thought of that whip might loosen their tongues a bit," Mitch answered.

The one on the ground wasn't up to any questioning yet, but the other one was more than willing to tell them what they wanted to know. Diego offered them a couple of women if they got rid of the bigwig in town. Mitch laughed. "You boys must mean Luke. You picked the wrong man."

"But they described the wife and her friend and you are walking with both of them."

"Only walking them home, someone mentioned unsavory characters in town and I guess that would be you two. I didn't want the ladies facing you on their own."

"Why not? Trying to rescue us? That there woman is one mean woman, look what she did to poor Lenny there. He ain't ever going to have a family now."

"You mean someone would want him any other time?" Temperance stuck in.

"Aw Lady. Old Lennie ain't so bad. We been traveling together many years and he always does his share."

"Like holding the insurance gun under a paper so it is a sure thing when you cause a fight?" she answered.

"Well, yeah."

"That isn't exactly a glowing endorsement of his sterling qualities for parenthood," she told him.

"Where is Diego staying or where are you supposed to meet him?" she asked.

"They're up at the old stone trail hut near the Pass, oof," he floundered from the kick good old Lennie delivered to his shin.

"Aww Lennie, don't be mad. They was going to use that whip on you some more." he whined.

Lennie moaned and rolled over, holding himself even tighter.

Nate and the other customer grabbed the two men and hustled them over to the makeshift jail. Temperance heard the men howl as they were put down in the hole. Nate yelled to shut up or he would tell everyone the building was open for use. Then Reggie and Gale joined in the fracas. Mitch hurried the women on up the hill. He, Luke and as many others as they could gather were going after Diego and Josh.

After the men left, Temperance had the women barricade the house. She felt the information was given a little too freely on the whereabouts of Josh and Diego. She told Grandfather her thoughts on it and he agreed. He took the old Sharps rifle up to the crow's nest on the roof. He would have a perfect view of the surrounding countryside from there.

They worked fast and in pairs, closing the ground floor shutters over the windows from outside, fastening them on the inside. The doors were locked up tight. Then she braced a chair under the knob on each door. She didn't

179

know whether or not Josh kept keys to the house after he was fired.

They kept a large pot of stew simmering on the stove so everyone could eat when they returned. The women took turns standing guard up with Fernando in the crow's nest. He refused to go downstairs until the men returned. He said he refused to allow women to stand guard while he rested.

They heard gunfire later in the day from the direction of the old stone hut. Everyone paused for brief prayers for their men and the townsmen that were helping.

After a few more hours, Temperance was ready to saddle up and go hunt down the men herself. A couple more hours after that and Charity was ready to go with her. Jasmine, Pearl and Sue Lee couldn't make up their minds whether or not they wanted to leave the safety of the house for the woods and on a horse, at that. They were not experienced horse people.

Fernando held firm. Luke expected them to be here, safe and sound so he didn't have to worry about them getting hurt or being taken hostage. Staying here was the best way they could help Luke and Mitch.

As the night was almost over, they could see horses coming through the brush under the trees up on the hill. They could not tell who it was, but Temperance recognized some of their horses.

Then the riders came into view and she saw Mitch leading another horse with a body draped over it. Dear Lord in Heaven, No.

She ran down the stairs, not waiting to see who else was coming and pulled the chairs away from the knobs. She opened the door and ran out the back of the house toward the men riding in.

A shot rang out from the trees behind the men and she saw Luke slowly falling toward the ground off the horse he was riding, behind Mitch. Then she was falling too and heard another shot just before losing consciousness. She never heard the boom of the old Sharps rifle in the crow's nest as Diego finally died. Then there was silence.

Chapter 19

When Temperance regained consciousness, she first reached for her belly and was reassured to still feel the swell of her child. Pain radiated from her other shoulder and she succumbed to the darkness again.

The next time, she held very still and willed each finger and toe to move, making sure she could feel them all, then she slowly opened her eyes without moving. There, in a cot near hers was Luke, looking back at her. He had a large bandage covering his shoulder and upper arm. He looked wonderful, he was alive. She smiled and dozed off to sleep again.

This was a restful healing sleep and she slept many hours before awakening yet again. Luke was asleep this time and she marveled at how beautiful his body was with just the sheet over his torso and his upper body showing to perfection in the glow of the sun through the window. The even rise and fall of his chest, even the fan of his lashes on his cheek was dear to her. She loved him.

She slowly sat up in her cot, wondering why they weren't both in their own bed, when she realized it would be far easier to take care of injured people downstairs in the formal parlor where they now were resting.

She carefully swung her legs over the side and sat still a while longer, waiting for the room to hold still. The small table beside the cot held a glass of water and she carefully raised it to her lips and drank. It was the most wonderful feeling, easing her dry mouth and soothing her throat. She thought she must have been sleeping with her mouth open to be so dry.

After sitting up a few minutes, she decided she really was too tired to get up, so laid back down and went back to sleep. When she awoke the next time, someone was sitting near her cot.

"You shouldn't have got up by yourself to get a drink. What if you had fell? You could have hurt yourself more."

Temperance opened her eyes again and looked into Charity's face, inches from her own.

"Hello to you, too. I didn't fall and I didn't get up, I just sat on the edge of the bed a bit then went back to sleep. How is Luke?"

"Luke will be fine. He is actually in better shape than you are. He has been a good patient so far, although he is a little testy about anyone taking care of him, instead of taking care of you. I think he is just about ready to try getting out of bed with some help. Do you want me to help you sit up with some pillows around you to help you stay upright?"

"Yes please. I feel like I have been ran over by a team of horses then they came back and ran over me a couple more times for fun."

Charity carefully helped her sit up on the bed and placed several large cushions around her to hold her upright with no strain.

Temperance relaxed against the cushions and watched Luke. He was still asleep but as she watched him, his eyes slowly opened and she was looking into the depths of his being.

Luke could not believe it, he was so sure he was going to lose Temperance that he was not even trying that hard to recover and there she was, looking at him, sitting up on her cot. He started to get up and almost fell trying to ignore the pain in his arm and shoulder.

Pearl came in as he was trying to get up and lit into him in her native language. He had no clue what she was saying, but the finger she kept shaking at him looked like she was going to use it as a weapon if he didn't stay put. He shrugged and pointed to Temperance, Pearl turned, saw Temperance was sitting up and rushed over to see if she needed anything.

Jasmine came in, carrying a tray with cups of broth and some early berries in honey. Temperance heard her tummy rumbling at the delicious odor of food and she really wanted a steak. Her imagination got a workout, as she sipped the broth. Luke drank his and asked where the steak was. She could have kissed him. Great minds think alike.

Charity brought them more broth, but included some of the meat chopped up in it. Temperance found that the water and broth helped her feel less light headed.

After they ate, they both wanted to move back to their own bed, but when the doctor dropped by, he advised against it. Any accidental bumps during the night would have them in agony again and could even reopen his careful stitching job.

Temperance had never met the man before as he was fairly new in town. He seemed pleasant and his hands were gentle as he checked her wound. He asked questions about her pregnancy and she decided he was probably a nice person. She had never been examined by a doctor and wasn't sure how to behave having a stranger touch her, even if it was only on her shoulder, checking the stitches.

"I think I can remove the stitches in both of you in a few more days. Everything seems to be healing up nicely and if you are very careful, you shouldn't have any problems from your injuries," he told them.

During the night, Temperance woke up to the sound of someone unlocking the front door.

"Who is there?" she called out.

Silence, then the door softly closed and she heard the sound of the lock reengaging.

The next morning, she forgot all about it and then visitors dropped in and by evening, she had put it entirely out of her mind.

The next evening, she again thought she heard the door being unlocked after everyone was asleep in the house. Then she remembered the night before. Who would be coming in the house at this time of night and why were they able to unlock the door?

The sound of footsteps somehow muffled filtered into the formal parlor where she and Luke were convalescing. The steps went up the stairs and she tried to follow the direction they turned at the top of the stairs. Then they slowed as they reached the door to the room she and Luke shared.

Temperance reached under her pillow for the small handgun Luke had given her several months ago.

She considered trying to wake Luke, but he was usually a sound sleeper and she was afraid she would give away their location if she called loudly enough to wake him.

She slowly eased herself upright and edged to the floor. Her first step was almost her last as she felt like her legs were made of soft rope. She found the crutch that had been left for her to use once she was allowed out of bed. She caught herself and inched toward the door. She had just reached the door and was still partially behind it when she heard steps coming back down the stairs. She eased herself down into a chair and waited.

She was partly behind the door where she could see through the crack and watched the person stop at the foot of the steps, then slowly proceeding toward the formal parlor. She could not tell who the man was, his hat was pulled low over his forehead and he had a kerchief over his lower face. Although the nights were not dark, the curtains were all pulled, keeping the house fairly darkened and not making it easy to identify the man.

As he neared the door to the parlor, Temperance steeled herself to shoot him as soon as he stepped through the door. She was afraid if she asked who he was, he might harm Luke before she could shoot if she waited.

Just as he almost reached the door, Temperance heard a door open upstairs and footsteps coming down the hallway toward the stairs. The man heard them too and whirled around, heading for the door. He looked familiar somehow, but Temperance couldn't place how she might know him. Maybe she had just seem him around town over the winter without actually knowing him. She hated to think a friend would do them harm.

Pearl came down the stairs, "Who was here? I just had a dream and as I was coming down to check on you, I heard the door, is everything alright? Why are you out of bed and sitting behind the door with a gun in your hand?"

"I don't know who it was. Someone has a key to the house and came in, I heard them go up to our room, then come back. I moved over here and was going to shoot him when he stepped into the room. I was afraid to make enough noise to wake up Luke. I didn't know what that person would do if he was in here and we were suddenly all awake."

By this time, Luke actually was awake and bewildered.
"Someone was in the house?"

"Yes, we need to change the locks or add some way to fasten then on the inside once we are ready for the night. As I heard the door unlock tonight, I remembered hearing it last night, too. I called out and they left, last night."

Everyone looked at her. She fidgeted a bit, "What? I forgot and went to sleep."

She found her legs would not cooperate when she wanted to go back to bed. She was suddenly very tired and was happy for the support the rest of the women provided as now everyone in the house was up and downstairs.

After she was settled in her bed again, she was asleep before the rest left the room.

The next morning, she got up again and found she was not quite as weak and wobbly. She managed to make it into the kitchen and was sitting at the table when Charity came in.

"Just what do you think you are doing?"

"I got tired of the same view. I would also like to wash up some, I feel like I have been wearing this gown for a week at least."

"That's only because you have been."

"What? Just how long have I been out? I thought it was only a day or two. No wonder I feel so weak. Now tell me exactly what happened?"

Charity told her that after she and Luke were shot, her grandfather had shot Diego from the crow's nest of the house. This time he would not recover. The other person with Diego had gotten away. He said Diego was the one with the rifle and did the shooting of her and Luke. Everyone rushed them into the house and got the doctor from town up to take care of them. The man being brought in was traveling with Josh and Diego, as he was shot while the posse closed in on them. They followed the others quite a ways, then gave up and headed home, only to have the ones they were chasing evidently turn right around and follow them back. No one knew who the dead man was. He had no papers of any sort on him. None of their group thought they had shot at him, so he must have been killed by Diego or Josh. It was all confusing.

Charity had the banked fire going and the water was soon warm enough to prepare a wash basin for Temperance who started freshening up while Charity went upstairs to find her another gown. She helped her into it and combed out her hair. Then she finished preparing breakfast as the other women wandered into the kitchen.

The yell from the parlor brought their attention back to Luke.

"Where is Temperance? What has happened? Someone help me get up, uh, please?"

Temperance stayed seated and the rest went in to see if they could help Luke get up and at least partly dressed. Soon they staggered into the kitchen with him draped over their shoulders, trying to walk and take as much of his weight off them as possible.

They made it to the bench close to the wall. He plopped down on the bench and a sheen of sweat covered his forehead from the effort.

Jasmine took the wash basin and dumped it, preparing fresh warm water and took it over to him. She bathed his back then handed him the cloth and he washed his face and as much as he could reach of his chest with one hand. Pearl was back with a fresh shirt for him to wear. They eased his bandaged arm into it and buttoned it for him. He felt a bit better by the time they were done and breakfast was ready. Fernando came down and groused about people not smart enough to stay in bed and heal up. Everyone ate in the kitchen, Luke on the bench and Temperance in the chair she had settled in. By the time the meal was done, they were more than ready to go back to their cots.

The women all breathed a sigh of relief when Mitch knocked on the door. They led him through to the kitchen and told him of the night's happenings. He thought a few minutes then said he would go pick up some supplies in town and fix the doors so no one could get in after they were fastened up for the night. Charity asked for his assistance first in getting the two patients back to their beds. He obliged, he and Fernando working together and both soon back on their own cots in the parlor. Luke asked that one of his pistols be brought in so he could keep it close at hand. He should at least be as well armed as his wife. Within minutes they were both asleep.

When Mitch returned after walking Charity to the Laundry and stopping at the store, he worked as quietly as possible on both doors, only resorting to hammering after he had both chiseled out quietly and ready for the deadbolt installation. Of course the hammering brought both Luke and Temperance wide awake. Both reached for their guns, then laughed that they were just a little bit jumpy.

Chapter 20

Mitch showed Jasmine, Pearl and Sue Lee how to work the new deadbolts. Luke and Temperance both made it out to see how to work them. These could not be unlocked from the outside at all, only by turning the latch on the inside.

Sometime during the night, Temperance thought she heard the door rattle, then a muted curse and steps going off the porch. Ha! The new locks worked.

The next day she mentioned what she had heard. "Why didn't you wake us up? Maybe we could have caught whoever it is."

"Oh, well, by the time I could hobble around and get anyone awake, do you think the person on the porch would just stand there and wait for me to get someone up, sounds reasonable."

"Alright, you've made your point," her grandfather grumped at her.

Temperance refused to stay in bed any longer. Luke felt the same way, so they assisted each other and were soon ready to sit on the porch a while. When Fernando came in from the glass growing house, he just shook his head and muttered as he walked on into the house. Charity was more vocal but by evening, Luke and Temperance were both ready to go in, eat and go back to bed.

From then on, there was no keeping them indoors. Soon Temperance was helping weed in the glass house. She only needed one hand and didn't have to bend over. There was a bench in there that she could sit on any time she felt the need to sit down.

Luke couldn't find any chores simple enough to do using only one hand. Barn chores needed both hands and so did anything to do with firewood. He ended up in the glass house with Temperance. Fernando grumbled but soon was engrossed with showing them how it all worked.

Since Temperance had started wearing fairly lose housedresses, no one noticed her increasing size. Luke knew and so did the other women in the house but Fernando didn't have a clue. No one else in town except Mattie knew either. Pregnancy was not a public process at this time and no one went out in public once it was noticeable. People's private lives were just that, private.

Fernando did not want to spend another winter here. However, he also didn't want to leave if his granddaughter was in danger. He asked Luke if they would like to accompany him on a trip to Europe. He would like to travel while he could still enjoy it. The new ocean liners made the trip so pleasurable that it would be nice to travel there, now. They could even stop and see her brothers if she desired. He silently shuddered at the thought.

Temperance was torn between wanting to travel and knowing if they did, she would soon be too large to be seen in decent company. The thought of having her child far

194

from home wasn't one she wanted to dwell on. Before Luke could say one way or the other, she thanked her grandfather and told him at any other time she would have jumped at the chance, but she just couldn't leave at present. She rubbed her waist lightly and hoped he would get the hint.

His eyes bugged a bit and he stepped back as though she might be contagious. "Oh, I see. That would definitely cause some inconvenience, wouldn't it? I think I will plan on leaving here for Valdez within the week and make better plans once I know the schedule of the ships from there."

Luke looked back and forth between them, not sure if he caught all the undercurrents of the exchange. Temperance turned to him and offered her arm to have him accompany her indoors.

"Do you folks ever just come out and say exactly what you want to say? I feel like there was an entire conversation going on there that I have no idea about."

"I was just letting Grandfather know he is going to be a Great Grandfather and it is probably best if we don't travel right now."

"Uh, alright. Why not just tell him?"

"It just isn't done. Not only are ladies not supposed to sweat, have legs or an opinion, but they are definitely not supposed to let anyone know they actually have physical relations resulting in a b-a-b-y."

"How do people think most of them have such large families then?"

195

"That is one of the wonders of the universe. Ladies don't do those sort of things and if she did, she certainly didn't enjoy it."

"Well, Lady Mine, shall we try going upstairs and see if we can manage some of that stuff no one talks about with us both crippled up on one side?"

They did make it upstairs, but before they could attempt their room, Charity burst through the entry door.

"Temperance, Luke, there is a group of men down at the store and I think they are robbing it. Not that you should go down there, but maybe if we get Fernando up in the crow's nest with the Sharps, maybe he can pick a few of them off and dang, I am going to have to learn to shoot better."

Fernando came in the back door and heard the last of this and started for the crow's nest, picking up the Sharps as he passed it hanging on the wall. Antonio and Jose came in the door right behind Charity. Each carried a large rifle. The men headed for the crow's nest.

As the gang robbing the store came out the door, the men in the crow's nest opened fire from their perch. Charity reloaded for the men as they fired. Temperance and Luke could only watch from the porch and saw one of the men sneak around behind the others and make his way down to the creek bank and headed their way. The cover afforded by trees and brush kept him out of sight of the men upstairs but Luke and Temperance could see him very well.

They each had their revolvers but were still too far away for complete accuracy with their injuries. The man kept his hat low and had a kerchief over his lower face. Temperance gasped and said she thought he was the man that came in the house the other night.

As he worked his way closer to the house, Luke kept him in his sights. Suddenly the man disappeared and did not come back into view.

They waited, keeping a watch of the area and around them, also, in case he dropped down and was creeping through the weeds on his belly. Nothing moved.

No more shots came from the crow's nest either, so finally they sat and faced different directions just in case he popped up somewhere near them.

When the men came downstairs from the crow's nest, Luke told them about the other man. They searched the area and found a place that looked like it might be the end of a tunnel. Where it came out would be anyone's guess.

No one wanted to go into it after an armed man. They did the next best thing, they searched every out building and the barn.

They built a large brush pile in the tunnel entrance and lit it, adding green branches and leaves as it burned. Soon a yell sounded from the barn and they saw dark smoke coming from the tunnel there. Now what? In the barn, Mitch found where a tunnel opened out in the grain room and one of the horses was missing and tack for it. The tracks looked like the horse was led away quite a distance before being mounted and rode away.

When Pearl went down in the cellar for supplies for dinner, she could smell a faint residue of smoke. She came up and mentioned it to Mitch. He took a larger lantern and went down into the cellar and searched around. He found a small seep of smoke filtering in through a very small crack in the wall. It would only require a small amount of digging to join this to the tunnel to the creek bank.

Luke was thinking hard when Mitch came back up from the cellar. "Where is the map we found last Fall with the woman's body?"

"I think it is in the library in the desk or up in your room with your important papers." Temperance told him.

"Could that be what the person coming in at night has been looking for? Is it a map of the old Russian compound that was here before I settled this town?" Luke asked.

Charity and Mitch went upstairs yet again looking for the map and papers.

Luke edged over to his desk and searched using only one hand and Temperance used her uninjured hand, so between them, they managed fairly well to search the entire desk.

No map was found. They tried sketching out the map as each one remembered it, but somehow none of the drawings looked anything like what they remembered. Sue Lee came in to see if she could bring in some refreshments and looked at their efforts. "No, that's not right" and she proceeded to sketch out a complete map with the notes on the bottom fairly accurately. She did not read or write well, but she could draw almost anything with a wonderful memory for detail. To her, the writing was just more of the picture.

Everyone looked at her in awe. She blushed and rushed back to the kitchen. She helped Pearl finish dinner preparations.

No one knew whether their visitor would attempt to come back and try gaining entrance to the house through the tunnel system or not, so they placed a heavy barrel over the trap door and took turns standing guard in the crow's nest so they could see anyone approaching that entrance. The one in the barn had another large barrel placed over it and several implements stacked on it to clatter and make nose if anyone attempted to move them.

No one slept very soundly and they were a grumpy looking lot the next morning. When Mitch showed up, they were still grumpy so he told them he would escort Charity to work then come back and help block off the tunnels. Charity asked if they should possibly search them first to see if there was anything of interest down there.

Fernando, Mitch and a couple of the men that sometimes worked for Luke took lanterns and started in the tunnel that still smelled faintly of smoke. Once they got farther underground, the tunnel forked into several branches and they realized the map gave a fairly good depiction of what they were looking at. Now they could determine where the house sat in relation to the tunnels and the barn, also. They went back upstairs to talk to Luke.

"Luke, who picked out exactly where everything was going to be built here, for the house and barn?"

"Josh, Gary and I walked around on this hill and looked it all over. We looked for the best views and least possibility that the area would end up needing to be torn up following

199

the gold in the valley floor. I made the final decision, I think."

"How did you pick exactly this hill to start on, why not the one just over a bit farther away from the workings?"

"One of the men, I don't remember if it were Josh or Gary that suggested close enough to keep an eye on the workings while still far enough away to not be in the way of those same workings," he replied.

"So, either you, Josh or Gary picked the site and then the exact placement of the buildings?"

"Yes, something like that, although the house isn't exactly where I put it on the sketches in relation to the trees we left in place for the yard. When I said something, I was told it was the easiest spot to make level without messing up those trees."

"Say, where is Gary this winter? I haven't seen him around for a while. I thought he was courting Mattie in a low key way." Mitch asked.

"He said he had to go downriver to help out his family this winter. They live in one of the villages closer to the coast, along the Yukon." Luke told him.

"So one of the three of you picked the building site and we can take you out of the mix. That leaves Josh or Gary. Why would either of them want the house over the tunnels and the barn over another one?" Mitch pondered.

"Well, it would give someone access at any time to the house and also an escape route, it they wanted, which it did, yesterday."

"I just can't see why anyone would want to access the house or maybe the cellar wasn't supposed to reach the tunnels. Remember, we did enlarge it a bit when we dug out starting soil for the glass house." Temperance put in.

"That's right. We did enlarge it and it still doesn't quit join the tunnel, it just gets some ventilation through a small hole between them. Maybe that tunnel needs searched to the end of it?" Luke said.

"Let's just build up a good fire at the mouth of the main tunnel tonight to keep it blocked for the night and the barrels over the other possible ways in and maybe you can sleep better and wake up in a better mood tomorrow. Then we can search farther into the system. The map shows a room at the end of the tunnel going near the cellar. Maybe it holds our answers." Mitch told them.

Chapter 21

The next day, Luke was feeling so much better he decided to go searching tunnels with Mitch. They covered his bandage with even more wrappings and a shirt, then a jacket.

He could barely move that arm with all the wrapping and covering, not that he wanted to move it much yet anyway. He stuck a handgun in his pants belt and they proceeded to the tunnel, scrapping all the ashes and small pieces of charred wood away.

Once they were in the tunnel a ways, it opened up fairly well and they could walk upright with their lanterns. When they reached the junction in the tunnels, they turned to the right, going past the cellar and on toward the room that showed on the map.

They were surprised to see that the room was blocked by a large heavy looking door across it that was barred on this side. Mitch lifted the bar and had it in his hand when he pulled open the door. A body charged out of the darkness, barreling into him and he was glad Luke had both lanterns as he now had someone on him, pummeling him. He brought up the bar and cracked the figure under the chin with it, knocking the person partially out.

Luke and Mitch stared in shock at the dirty, bearded disheveled figure of Gary OldMan laying on the floor in front of them.

Gary slowly opened his eyes and rubbed his chin. "Luke? Mitch? Where did you come from? I thought it was the rotten sonofagun that put me in here. At least he didn't starve me, but he left very little and not enough candles to keep burning much each day. I sure am glad to see friendly faces," he sat up a little straighter.

Luke still wanted to see the room under his house, so they turned and walked back in the room Gary had hoped to never see again.

The walls were reinforced and the room was quite large. Luke figured it went clear under the main family parlor. The dirt overhead would have muffled any sounds made down here. The lanterns were brighter than the lone candle Gary burned once in a while and he could make out more detail of his dungeon.

As they looked it over, Luke wondered why it didn't smell all that bad if Gary had been in here most of the winter or even a couple of weeks? Gary noticed him sniffing the air.

"I managed to dig out a hole over near the wall and as I used it, I put some dirt back in it, then moved and made another hole when that one got fairly full. I couldn't stand the thought of living in here very long in my own filth. I imagine I smell pretty bad anyway without a bath for so long," he said.

As Luke walked around the room, he tapped on the walls and found several built in niches with removable sections of wall over them. Gary just stared.

"I never would have even thought to look for something like that," he told them.

Each hole had a leather wrapped parcel in it that was extremely heavy for their size. Mitch and Gary carefully lifted them out of their holes.

They carefully started carrying their find to the part of the wall that Luke thought opened into the cellar. He tapped along the wall and found where it crumbled in. He started knocking the dirt away from the small hole, enlarging it enough that they could place the wrapped parcels in the cellar. Then they carried all they found in the rest of the walls and everything was placed in the cellar. Luke stepped through the hole into the cellar and Mitch and Gary proceeded out the end of the tunnel. They would find some shovels and cover this hole up for good. Leaving the tunnel under the house and the room, even leaving the tunnel to the barn intact, possibly.

Mitch and Gary pulled on some of the old timbers out from the walls near the opening as they neared it, and could hear the dirt trickling down and increasing in volume as they went on out the opening. As they looked back, the tunnel looked quite well blocked just from that small amount of improvisation.

When Mitch and Gary came in, the others were astonished to see Gary and looking so unkempt. He usually always took very much pride in being clean shaven and not allowing himself to get slovenly like some of the men around camp did. They were even more surprised when the men went straight through to the cellar and rolled the barrel off it. When they opened the cellar door and

Luke started handing up the lighter wrapped objects everyone was full of questions. As the parcels were set on the floor, they clunked even wrapped in leather.

Temperance opened one and gasped as she looked at the gold chalice in her hand. It was ornate and lovely and gleamed in the light through the window. Everyone turned and looked.

They slowly uncovered all the items already lifted up and it was obvious this was all the Holy artifacts used in a Russian Orthodox Church.

Mitch went down into the cellar to help with the larger heavier items that needed at least two good hands to lift up. There were a couple of very large gilded icons, folded up, that were breathtaking when set up on the kitchen table. The largest of the icons was the last item lifted out of the cellar. When they opened the side panels and set it on the table it glowed in the light. The gold on it was amazing and the detail in the painting took on a life of its own.

"Where can we put it to keep it safe?" Temperance asked.

"I am amazed they are in such good condition. I would have thought the wood in the icons would have drawn dampness after all these years," Gary said.

Everyone turned to look at him. "Do you know anything about them, Gary?"

"I have heard rumors. They were stolen from one of the Churches downriver a few years ago. There are still several Russian Orthodox Churches in Alaska and they will be so pleased to get them back. Oh, you are planning on returning them, aren't you?" he asked.

Fernando walked in from where he had been keeping watch and asked if he was ever going to be relieved, he was getting tired up in the crow's nest. Then his eyes fell on the holy treasures on the table and he hurriedly crossed himself.

He gazed in awe at the lovely items displayed on the table and asked where they were located and what was to be done with them.

Gary offered to contact his priest downriver and let them handle it from there, if they so choose. He suggested they pack everything to one of the upstairs rooms and lock them in. There really was not a secure place for them anywhere in town. Fernando, Mitch and Gary carried the items up the stairs and secured them in one of the spare bedrooms.

Gary was finally ready to get cleaned up and something to eat that hadn't been left in the cavern for weeks. He looked a bit pale after shaving off his beard and washing up, having been underground a while. Mitch walked down to let Mattie know what happened and she came back up the hill with him. She told Charity she didn't know how much the man meant to her until he wasn't around any more.

Tears filled her eyes as she looked at him. He had lost a bit of weight and his clothes were filthy. She asked if he would like to come down to the laundry and soak a while and she would wash his clothes and find some he left there that certainly were ready to change in to.

He accepted and they walked back down the hill together. There would be time for more explanations later. No one had any answers as Gary had not named the person that left him in the cellar or how he happened to get involved, either. There were far more questions than answers.

After Gary and Mattie left, the others sat around the table in the kitchen discussing everything.

"So, where do we go from here? We still don't know who, what or why, although those treasures certainly could be the why." Temperance asked.

"Does anyone here know anything about the robbery Gary spoke about? What kind of person robs a Church? Those are priceless and no one would ever receive even half their value if they tried to sell them off anywhere." Charity said.

Mitch said he thought he had hear rumors about it when he first moved up here, but he couldn't remember any of the particulars. He thought there was some sort of scandal tied to it and everyone thought it was some kind of inside job.

"Truly? An inside job in a Church? How could that be?" Charity wondered. "What was it, a fake Priest? Or was the altar boy really a midget thief?"

She shrugged and said "Well, I just don't know how a Church robbery could possibly be an inside job."

"Maybe the cleaning lady mentioned where certain items of value were stored to someone in her home and they did it," Temperance put in.

"Maybe we can wait and ask Gary. He seemed to know more about it." Luke said.

"Well where is the fun in that? One of our ideas might be right." Temperance laughed up at him.

The next day, Temperance and Pearl were weeding in the garden when Mitch walked up the hill. The sun was hot enough both women welcomed an excuse to quit and go in the house for a break.

They found lunch ready when they got indoors and Temperance was feeling the effects of her injury. Weeding is not an easy chore at any time and she was feeling like maybe she overestimated her degree of recuperation. When she plopped down on a chair in the kitchen, she felt like it was going to take a block and tackle to lift her back up. Maybe she would just put her head down on the table and sleep a while, too.

Jasmine plonked a plate down near her head and the delicious odors roused her enough to sniff appreciatively. Her stomach rumbled and she decided maybe she was not quite ready to sleep the rest of the afternoon away. Maybe later, after she ate.

During lunch, Mitch said he talked a while with Gary last night and again this morning. Gary said his assailant wore some sort of cover over his lower face and his hat pulled down so low, he was never completely sure who the man was. He was almost positive it was Josh, but not positive enough to swear out a warrant. Gary looked none the worse for wear for having been kept prisoner so long. Must be his naturally tanned skin.

Luke and Mitch kept the barrel over the cellar door just in case there was another way into the tunnel since it now came directly into the house. The women felt better about that and the new deadbolts on the doors. No one else knew about the new deadbolts though and they were keeping it that way.

That night, Temperance woke up and thought she heard someone fiddling with the lock on the door, then a short while later, the back door rattled a bit, also. She smiled to herself in her half sleep and went back to sleep. She thought they could move back to their bedroom soon.

The next morning, before too many people started moving around in the house, Temperance and Luke moved all the treasures from the locked room into the closet in their own bedroom. Then they covered the pile of wrapped bundles with folded blankets and pillows. She was right, they were well enough to manage the stairs fairly easily and tonight they would finally sleep in a real bed again. They relocked the room the treasures had been stored in. No use letting anyone know they had been moved.

They collapsed on the bed and lay there with their arms touching. It felt so good to lay back on a comfortable mattress. Those cots were not so great for long term use as beds. She, for one, was sick and tired of hers. Before she knew it, someone was tapping at their door and Sue Lee stuck her head around the corner, laughing and waking them up.

"Time for lunch, lazy bones, you missed breakfast because no one knew where you were."

Temperance stretched and almost smacked Luke. He grabbed her hand and they sat up together, yawning and stretching.

"I didn't know just how much I missed this bed until just now. I don't think I ever want to use a cot again," Luke said.

Temperance laughed and told him she had been thinking the very same thing. They got up and walked down the stairs for lunch.

At work in the Laundry, Mattie asked Charity if she thought Gary was on the up and up. Charity wasn't sure exactly what Mattie was asking her.

"What do you mean, Mattie? I think he is a very nice man. He seems to always be around when we needed help."

"That's what I mean. Don't it seem a bit odd to you that he always just happens to be in the area just when he is needed? It don't seem quite right to me. I know I missed him while he was gone, but I didn't notice that until he got back, so I probably am not actually in love with him like I thought I might be. Does that make sense to you?"

"Now that you mention it, you are right and yes, that does make sense to me. How about we keep an eye on him a bit better for a while. If you feel something is wrong, you are probably right." Charity told her.

They heard steps slowing on the boardwalk outside and went back to work, folding clothes and talking about what a dry summer it had been so far.

Gary came in the door with a can of fresh blueberries. "I found a hillside where they are just finally starting to ripen. Maybe you ladies would enjoy these?" Doffing his hat to them, he went back out the door.

"See? He is always just right there. But fresh blueberries, he does know how to ingratiate himself, don't he?" Mattie said.

Charity laughed and plopped a blueberry in her mouth. It wasn't totally ripe but the flavor was intense. "These would make a wonderful batch of dumplings."

"What are you waiting for, Girl, there is the little kitchen and enough supplies for dumplings. We can have some for lunch, even if it is a bit late."

Charity started the blueberries cooking as she mixed the thick batter for the dumplings. Soon the smell permeated the entire building and they heard steps slow, falter then head back for the door. Mitch stuck his head in.

"Is that blueberries I smell?"

"Yes, Mitch and they are almost done. Care to join us for lunch?"

He placed his arm behind his back and walked sideways into the building, "Oh, you are twisting my arm something awful. I'll eat them."

"That may be the worst playacting I've ever seen, but alright, you may still have some."

Chapter 22

Josh found a stable to keep and care for the horse he was riding and caught the riverboat heading downriver. When he reached the first village that had a Russian Orthodox Church, he disembarked. When he reached the Church, he found the Priest in the Sanctuary and waited for him to finish what he was doing.

The Priest turned and saw Josh and came toward him. "Have you had any luck finding your sister and the man you searched for?" he asked.

"Yes, Father. My sister was killed by the man and he is now locked away in an underground room that he held me captive in for several weeks I think. I am not sure of the amount of time."

The Priest took his hand and turned toward his home. "You look starved, you must eat. We have some fine fresh salmon my housekeeper prepared for lunch today. We will talk while you eat."

Over a large meal set out by the silent housekeeper, the men discussed how to go about searching for the stolen artifacts.

"Is there any way that you could get away and come with me for a while to search? I know they must be somewhere in that tunnel but now it is owned by a wealthy man and I am not sure how he will react to my being around. I did some stupid things and he fired me and kicked me out. I deserved it."

"I will send a message down river for someone to come take over here a while until we return. Then we can catch the riverboat due to stop here in a couple of hours and go back to this town of Paradise. I will bring my supplies to show who I am, and papers to identify myself, also. Now I will hurry and get this letter on the boat before it leaves." So saying, the Priest hurried over to his desk and started writing. He sanded the paper and folded it. He affixed his seal on the heavy paper. Josh had never seen anything like it. He thought all that went out of style a long time ago.

He took the letter back to the riverboat and the Captain assured him he would deliver it for the Father.

When Josh returned to the Church, Father Dimitris was ready to go. He had a large satchel bag and a smaller sack that contained food for the trip. They walked back down to the river bank as the riverboat headed upstream pulled in to restock firewood. The Father purchased their fares and they found a place to sit where they could watch all the activity of loading the boat with wood for the boilers.

The loaders were fast and soon they were on their way. Since it was light all night, they didn't have to stop and tie up like they did later in the Fall to keep from running into sandbars and sweepers. With the heavy river silt, the channels changed, sometimes overnight and the dry summer had the river levels falling so boats still managed to catch a sandbar once in a while. This trip they were lucky, no sandbars where they should not be.

When they reached the village where the horse was stabled, Josh worried that they should have brought another horse. Father Dimitris told him not to worry, they would be fine.

When they reached the stable, the hostler asked if they were headed toward Paradise as he had a horse that needed returned and didn't have anyone headed that way at present. Father Dimitris smiled and told him they would be happy to deliver the other horse. Soon they were on their way, back to Paradise.

As they rode down the hill toward Luke's home, they saw Luke out near the barn and Josh hallooo'd him to let him know they were coming in. Luke stood there in astonishment as the man he had been blaming for everything that had gone wrong here rode up and stepped down from one of his horses. He looked extremely thin and very pale but sunburned.

"Nice of you to return my horse, Josh. What all do you have to say for yourself?"

"Luke, I owe you a big apology, not just for the horse but many other things, too. I would like you to meet Father Dimitris. His Church is the Church downriver that was robbed many years ago."

Father Dimitris stepped down from his horse. He handed the reins to Josh.

"I'm not sure exactly who this horse belongs to, Luke. The hostler in Rampart said he belonged to someone here in Paradise and asked us to return him."

"Oh, he is my horse too and I was wondering how you came by him. Someone took him a few nights ago, the

216

same night Gary disappeared. Nice of them to see that he got back to me."

"Luke, many years ago, when my sister and I first came to Alaska, we worked around the Church downriver and she soon became the housekeeper for the house and cleaned the Church, also. I took off and my sister fell for someone that she thought was the answer to all her prayers. She wanted a home and a family most of all in life. She was sadly mistaken. The man convinced her to run away with him and told her to meet him out beyond the little village late one night. She did. He had some pack horses loaded down and one extra for her to ride. Many days later, she found out he had the holy icons she had proudly shown him one day while she cleaned them. He had stolen everything of value from the Church. She hid the treasure and icons in some safe place. She repacked the packs with stones, then she confronted him. He laughed at her and left her standing out there in the tundra. She finally managed to make her way back to the village but was very ill for quite a while."

"Then she found out she had lost a baby while she was ill. It snapped her last thread with reality and she set out for revenge on the man that had deceived her and caused her to lose a precious small life. She finally trailed the man to Paradise, but before she could confront the man in public, he killed her. That body up on the hill was my sister. She should have had letters and a map. If the man found them, he now has the property stolen from the Church. She said the items were somewhere here around Paradise and laughed about someone building over them. I saw the map once and read her letters but the man didn't know how to read Polish."

Luke stood there in shock. Josh sounded sincere and the Priest standing there in his garments looked very much exactly how a Priest should look. Josh couldn't have known the items were found and moved, so he might be telling the truth.

Antonio was working in the barn, so Luke called him over and asked if he would please take care of the horses for them. Antonio walked back to the barn leading the horses and Father Dimitris now carried his bag and Josh carried the remaining sack of food. Luke took them in the house and called to Temperance. He was going to have to talk fast before she could practice her whip skills on Josh again.

When Temperance walked into the hall and saw Josh and the Priest standing there, she didn't know whether to take on Josh or curtsy to the Priest. Good manners finally surfaced and she curtsied to the Priest. He blessed her and she smiled at him. Then she started to turn on Josh. Luke caught her and held her firmly against him and whispered in her ear. "Hush and listen to him first. Then if you still want to, go ahead."

He released her and she flounced ahead of them on into the kitchen, telling Luke to seat their guests in the parlor. She asked Jasmine to help her prepare a tray to take into the parlor for their guests. As she thought about it, she was intrigued by Luke asking her to refrain from skinning Josh alive. Just what was the story he was going to tell and should she believe him?

After the men were served and she helped herself to some refreshments, Josh retold them his story. The other women had come in and were seated around the room listening, also. No one interrupted him as he told them his story.

Luke told the Priest he would be welcome to spend the night if he wanted as this place was probably more comfortable than Josh's old cabin. Josh asked if he could bunk out in the barn as he didn't think he would have a very long life if anyone else knew he was back. He told them he had spent some of the winter under this house as a prisoner and really didn't enjoy it a bit. He was still trying to catch up on his eating and was certainly enjoying the refreshments supplied while he talked. He still looked quite gaunt and pale where he wasn't sunburned.

Luke turned over in his mind the difference in how Josh looked, even after having been out of the room underground for several days and how Gary had looked, even one day after his stay under the house. Josh's appearance bore out his story far better than Gary's did. He would talk to Temperance and the other women and Mitch about it later.

Father Dimitris turned out to be a delightful houseguest. Fernando was enjoying himself debating the differences in Russian Orthodox and Catholic practices. Their exchanges were lively and full of interesting information that Luke found very informative. He decided that if Father Dimitris was a fake, he was indeed a very well educated one in the Church. Fernando told them he had been scheduled to enter the priesthood when his older brother was killed and he became the heir. He had spent his youth studying for the Church. So he was very well informed also.

Josh was in the kitchen the next day and Father Dimitris was up on the crow's nest with Fernando when two horses with riders came down the hill toward the house from the north. One was dressed as a Priest and Gary rode the other horse.

Father Dimitris came quietly down the stairs and went into the kitchen with Josh. They sent the young women upstairs as they didn't know how dangerous this was going to become.

Temperance answered the door and was so startled she almost let the presence of the other Priest slip. She invited the two men into the house and seated them in the formal parlor. She ran to the back door and yelled for Luke but he was not close by and didn't hear her. He had walked down to see Mitch.

She came back into the parlor and asked if they would care for some refreshments, and the Priest said he really just wanted to recover the treasure and be on his way, he was a busy man. Temperance immediately stiffened her back and told him she was not in the habit of conducting her husband's business. Would they like some refreshments while waiting for him to come back? Gary shook his head at the priest.

"We would love some refreshments, it has been a hot dusty ride and I for one would like some of that delicious wine you keep."

"I'm sorry Gary, we haven't made any yet this year. The berries are ripening but we have only managed to pick enough to make jam, not even enough for packing in sugar for cooking all winter. The wine is the last thing we make after the berries are far sweeter than they are right now." She turned and walked back into the kitchen and hid the bottle of wine sitting on the table.

"I didn't lie, don't look at me that way. I said we had not made any yet this year and we have not. That is from last year," she whispered fiercely to Josh and the Priest. "That man with Gary is wanting the stuff we found and he is getting impatient. Josh, could you manage to get down the hill and speed Luke up getting home? If you go out the back and around the other side of the house he shouldn't see you go from the parlor windows."

She quietly let Josh out the back door, then latched it again and turned to preparing some refreshments. There was some cake and a cooling drink Jasmine made from some leaves she found growing along the creek. She prepared the tray and then hoped her sore shoulder would allow her to carry it to the parlor.

She set the tray down on the table and only spilled a very small amount of the drink. The small plates of cake slices and the cups of liquid were soon placed around on the small tables by the sofa the men were seated on. She prepared one for herself and perched on the edge of her chair. There was a pistol just under the edge of the cushion by her hand. She had left it there when she moved back upstairs and never got around to putting it anywhere else. She slowly maneuvered it into her apron pocket.

She soon heard Luke at the front door and hoped Josh went back around to the back and the Priest let him in.

When Luke entered the room, she smiled brightly at him and handed him a plate of cake. He seated himself closer to the two men. Temperance heard a small sound and glanced toward the stairs to suddenly see Jasmine holding the shotgun aimed at the two men in her parlor. From the angle they were sitting, they could not see what was behind them, so she smiled slightly and relaxed a bit.

Luke noticed her relaxing and thought it was because he was now home. He smiled also just thinking that she respected him and his ability to defend her that much.

Gary and the Priest started to worry. Why were these two smiling? They were so sure the gold would just be handed over and they could be on their way. Luke was here now, they didn't have time for any more silly pieces of cake and some lady drink that no man in his right mind would drink unless he had to.

"So, your wife wouldn't hand over the stuff and we need to be going, so if you will just hand it over, we can get it packed and be on our way," the priest told Luke. "I'm all for women knowing their places, but she refused to let us have them until you got back."

Luke could see the smile fade and be replaced by fury. He wasn't sure just what she was going to do, but she certainly wasn't going to meekly accept that.

"Gary, you never did introduce your friend here. I have fed you and given you drink for your thirst, the least you could do is introduce us," she smiled sweetly at Gary.

Uh-oh, Luke thought, it is going to be worse than I expected.

222

"This is the Priest from downriver I was telling you about." Gary said.

"Yes, I understand that, so what is his name? He surely isn't just called Priest?"

"Uh, his name is uh, Thomas. That's it, he is Thomas"

Temperance turned to the fuddled looking man behind Gary.

"Welcome to my home, Father Thomas`, have you been in Alaska long? Where did you study?" she waited, smiling sweetly.

"Uh, I've lived in Alaska almost 20 years. I was here long before the Gold Rush started. I studied at priest school back home," he muttered.

"And where would home be?" she held her hands clasped in front of her in the folds of her apron, like a demure little housewife.

Before Luke could move, Gary grabbed Temperance and held her in front of him with a knife near her throat.

"Enough of this nonsense. Get the parcels and we'll be on our way. Luke, you go get the parcels and I will hang onto the little wife here, and keep her company."

Luke watched in fascinated horror as his sweet little wife, sank her teeth into Gary while bringing up the pistol held in her clasped hands and shot him through the shoulder and the sound of breaking glass as the bullet went on through his shoulder and into something else.

The boom of the shotgun inside the house temporarily deafened them all and the man near Gary fell to the floor and Gary shuddered as the blast finished him off. Then the clatter of the shotgun hitting the floor and a shaken Jasmine apologizing for shooting so badly and dropping the gun but it kicked too hard. Fernando rushed to her side and helped her back up. He leaned the now reloaded shotgun within easy reach and came into the formal parlor.

"So, Granddaughter, you still have not learned to let your man rescue you and be suitably impressed by his skill in keeping you safe?" he smiled at her. Luke looked at Temperance and smiled at her.

"I wouldn't have her any other way. She is perfect."

Chapter 23

Father Dimitris sat at the kitchen table and looked over the cache of recovered treasures.

"I can't believe they are all here. Ilena was such a sweet young woman and I felt so sorry that she was involved in any way, but I never thought she stole them," he told Josh.

"All she was ever guilty of was having a tender heart and believing the sweet words a con man whispered in her ear. When I return home, we will hold a Mass for her. She did one last good deed, she hid them in a safe place and wrote the confession in Polish. You are probably one of the few men in Alaska Territory that can read it," he continued.

Josh turned to Luke and Temperance, "I owe you both a bigger apology. I was using my worry for my sister as an excuse for drinking and slowing down construction here while you were gone, Luke. I liked getting the easy money while trying to figure out how to find my sister. I never once thought Gary had anything to do with her or the theft of the Church property. I owe you about 2 months' worth of work. If you don't mind, I will work it off on repairing the tunnel and making the entrances better hidden. You never know when they might come in handy. I can work on them when no one is around, if you would rather not have them be common knowledge."

Luke and Temperance looked at each other and both nodded at the same time. "Sounds good to us."

Josh was going to escort Father Dimitris back home with his treasure. Then he would return and begin work.

Charity came home from the Laundry and stopped at sight of Josh, in the kitchen. Mattie had come home with her and Mitch escorted both ladies up the hill. The sudden clog of bodies in the doorway made Temperance start laughing again. Jasmine was seated near the sink and she was smiling, also. Her dismay at not shooting as straight as she planned and then dropping the gun was forgotten at the sight of the three people crammed in the doorway.

"What did we miss out on?" Charity asked.

Mattie's eyes widened at the sight of all the treasures spread out on the table. "My word, I have never seen such beautiful things. Is this what all the fuss has been about?"

"Yes, Senora," Fernando's smooth deep voice answered behind her. "This is what has caused all the fuss and pain. Greed does bad things to people that otherwise would be decent. Anytime someone schemes to get something that doesn't belong to him, it never turns out well."

Mattie turned and looked up into his deep brown eyes and smiled at the handsome older man. "That's a fact."

www.ingramcontent.com/pod-product-compliance
Lightning Source LLC
Chambersburg PA
CBHW060638260626
47161CB00008B/2911